MURDER GOES ROUND AND ROUND

ALSO BY HUGH PENTECOST

Pierre Chambrun Mystery Novels

Nightmare Time
Remember to Kill Me
Murder in High Places
With Intent to Kill
Murder in Luxury
Beware Young Lovers
Random Killer
Death After Breakfast
The Fourteen Dilemma
Time of Terror
Bargain with Death
Walking Dead Man
Birthday, Deathday
The Deadly Joke
Girl Watcher's Funeral
The Gilded Nightmare
The Golden Trap
The Evil Men Do
The Shape of Fear
The Cannibal Who Overate

Pierre Chambrun Short Stories

Murder Round the Clock

MURDER
GOES ROUND AND ROUND

A

PIERRE CHAMBRUN

MYSTERY

by Hugh Pentecost

Dodd Mead & Company

New York

First Edition

1 2 3 4 5 6 7 8 9 10

Library of Congress Cataloging-in-Publication Data

Pentecost, Hugh, 1903–
Murder goes round and round: a Pierre Chambrun mystery / by Hugh
Pentecost. — 1st ed.
p.   cm.
I. Title.
PS3531.H442M794   1988
813'.52—dc19   88-16165
ISBN 0-396-08952-6

Part One

1

I wouldn't have believed it if I hadn't heard and seen it. Toby March has a reputation in this country and abroad as an extraordinary jazz musician, both as a vocalist and an instrumentalist. When he and his supporting cast were booked into the Blue Lagoon, the glamorous nightclub in the Hotel Beaumont, New York's top luxury hotel, every inch of space was sold out for two weeks, long before a single note had been played or sung.

I was partly responsible for booking Toby March into the Beaumont, although I'd never heard him perform or talked business with him. I am Mark Haskell, public-relations director for the Beaumont, working for and with the hotel's legendary manager, Pierre Chambrun. Chambrun suggested I try to sign up Toby March for a stay in the Blue Lagoon. March's reputation was a guarantee to smash all box-office records. I never got to talk to March or to meet him. The business was handled by Frank Pasqua, March's manager, a bright-eyed, young Italian-American who could have sold tea to the Chinese. Toby March was brand-new to me until that opening Saturday night. I crowded into a corner of the Blue Lagoon for the second show that night, which started at midnight. When the show was over at about one-thirty, I was completely sold. Toby March was everything people had said he was and more. There was one grim and bizarre thing about that performance. There was no way that Toby March could have known, any more than I could have, that that was to be his last performance ever.

I had been warned by Frank Pasqua not to use the words "imitate" or "imitation" in my press releases about Toby March. Toby "recreated" famous jazz singers and instrumentalists. In that last performance, I heard Frank Sinatra, Tony Bennett and his love affair with San Francisco, and Sammy Davis, Jr., as vocalists, Benny Goodman on the clarinet, Harry James on the trumpet, Teddy Wilson on the piano, and Lionel Hampton on the vibes. March didn't do anything in the way of make-up to make himself look like the person whose music he was "recreating." But if you closed your eyes and listened and then looked up at the stage, you would have been shocked not to see Old Blue Eyes up there on the stage in person. March tried to stay anonymous so that his own identity wouldn't interfere with what he was "recreating." As a matter of fact, he blotted out his own appearance by wearing a black silk mask that covered his forehead, eyes, upper cheekbones, and nose. His press releases showed only pictures of the masked man. When I watched March's performance that first Saturday night, I had no idea what the star performer looked like, nor was I tempted to guess that anyone but Sinatra, or Goodman, or Hampton was behind that mask when their music was being "recreated." I was to learn later what lengths March had gone to to keep from being recognized as himself. Having watched him for an hour and a half, I might not have known him if I'd passed him on the street the next day. Of course, I wasn't going to pass him the next day, because by then he wasn't going to be in the land of the living.

Pierre Chambrun, French born, educated around the world by a nomadic father, is now ruling his own kingdom in New York City. That kingdom is the Hotel Beaumont, which I suppose you could call a small city within a city. The Beaumont has its own police force, its own hospital, its own bars, restaurants, shops, its own theater for the showing of live or filmed performances, and offices for its own lawyers, doctors, and stockbrokers. If you were a guest, I can't think of anything you might want that Chambrun's world could not provide.

I can't tell you that the Beaumont was free from crime, but the crimes that took place there over the years were crimes of passion, person-to-person violences. Organized criminal operations, such as the sale and distribution of drugs, large-scale confidence games, financial wheelings and dealings, simply didn't happen because The Man, Pierre Chambrun, was too watchful, too clever, I might almost say too psychic, for anything like that to get a foothold in his world. "When I don't know what's going on in my hotel," I've heard him say, "it will be time for me to quit."

Chambrun didn't know what was happening in his hotel in the early hours of the Sunday morning following Toby

March's Saturday-night opening in the Blue Lagoon. But, of course, there is no such thing as quitting in the steel-wire fiber of The Man. He would only have quit if he hadn't been properly prepared, if some part of the Swiss-watch functioning of his world had broken down. Even if he were psychic, Chambrun couldn't have foreseen what was going to happen on that Sunday morning. He would only think of quitting if he failed to see a violent criminal put behind bars.

Chambrun, short, stocky, yet elegant in his movements, could have been played to perfection by that late, great actor, Claude Rains. I have never, in all the time I've worked for him, found him caught off guard, trapped outside the image he presented of cultivated self-control. But believe me, this was a "perfect gentleman" with whom you wouldn't have wanted to cross swords.

Every day, Monday through Saturday, I have a regular routine with The Man. I report to his office at exactly nine o'clock. He will be drinking his first after-breakfast cup of coffee—Turkish coffee—seated at his carved Florentine desk, going over the list of yesterday's new Beaumont guests. On Sundays, the regular time schedule is changed. Life has been active in the Beaumont until the early hours of Sunday morning, and Chambrun and I meet in his penthouse on the roof of the hotel at about one o'clock in the afternoon.

On that Sunday afternoon, the time that this story really begins, our conversation began with a discussion of Toby March's opening in the Blue Lagoon the night before. Of course, I had been there for the second show and had seen it. Chambrun, anchored in his office by some operational problems, had only heard it over his intercom system.

"Audience seemed to be happy with it," Chambrun said.

"Hysterically happy," I said.

"It's amazing how well he gets away with it," Chambrun said. "He can't look like any of the performers whose music he 'recreates.' Some are white, some are black, fat or thin."

"He doesn't look like anybody, including himself. He wears a mask."

"Off stage as well as on?"

"That's what I'm told," I said. "I've never seen him without it. Frank Pasqua, who handles his promotion as well as his business affairs, has worked for him ever since he started this musical act, and he says March never lets anyone see him without the mask."

"He has to take a shower now and then or wash his hair," Chambrun said.

"He doesn't have to invite you or me to watch."

"Women?"

"Whatever his private life is, he hasn't let it be open to the public," I said.

"There has to be someone who knows what he looks like," Chambrun said. "He's a middle-aged man. He's only been doing this act of his for five years."

"The people he knew before he went public with his act are the people he has to hide from," I said.

"If what he really looks like was circulated, his act might not work. Right?"

"Right," I said. "The way he works, masked, there is no reason for the audience to think of anyone but the person they are hearing. Behind that mask must be Frank Sinatra, or Sammy Davis, Jr., or Benny Goodman. No one must not believe that in order for the act to work. No one must know that 'good old Johnny,' or whatever his real name is, is behind that mask hiding who he really is and what he really looks like. That's the name of his game."

"It sounds more like a master criminal trying to hide from the world, rather than a top-flight entertainer who needs to attract attention to his act," Chambrun said.

"To his act but not to himself," I said.

At that moment the door to Chambrun's living room was thrown open and Jerry Dodd, head of the Beaumont's security organization, charged in. Jerry, a short, wiry, intense little man, a former FBI agent, was free to come and go at will.

"There's hell to pay downstairs, boss," Jerry said to Chambrun.

"What kind of hell?"

"Seventeen C, Toby March's suite," Jerry said.

"Now what?"

"The maid on seventeen took some clean linens to March's suite," Jerry said. "The place was wrecked."

" 'Wrecked.' Wrecked how?"

"As if someone had taken a baseball bat and smashed chairs, tables, lamps. It turns out not to have been a bat but the iron poker from the fireplace tools. But that's just the beginning, boss. In the bedroom and bathroom, it looks as if there'd been a pigsticking. Blood everywhere—on the bedspread, on the rug, on the bath mat."

"And March himself?"

"No sign of him," Jerry said. "I've had to notify the police."

"Of course."

Bringing in the police would produce the kind of notoriety

Chambrun hated for his hotel. I knew he would have chosen to handle the beginning of the investigation himself, so that there could be some kind of sensible explanation before the police and the press made a sensation of it. But Jerry Dodd knew his job, and had felt the situation was serious enough to get moving on his own.

"Let's get down there," Chambrun said. "You locate Frank Pasqua, March's manager. He's in 17D, the room adjoining the suite."

"Not there," Jerry said. "One of the musicians told me that after a Saturday-night performance, March's people are free to go their own way. Pasqua didn't have to leave word where he might be going. 'Some dame somewhere,' his friend suggested."

"Wreckage" was a gentle word for what we found in March's suite. Chairs and tables smashed to pieces, table lamps shattered.

The bloody mess in the bedroom and bath was stomach-turning. It was hard to imagine that anyone subjected to that kind of violence could have survived.

The police arrived just as we were walking back into the living room. The officer in charge was a Lieutenant Herzog. I knew him by sight from the local precinct but not from any personal dealings. He was a tall, fair-haired, intense-looking guy, about forty, I'd guess.

"Somebody didn't like somebody," Herzog said. "The person who called in mentioned blood."

"That was me, hotel security, Lieutenant," Jerry said. "Come with me. I'll show you."

The moment the two detectives left Chambrun and me alone, the front doorbell sounded. Chambrun gestured to me to see who it was. The news was obviously out. Facing me was Doc Partridge, the hotel's house physician, a tall, gray-haired old man, who'd been Chambrun's doctor forever. Behind him in the hallway were three of March's musicians, Mrs. Kniffin, the housekeeper, and a maid.

"The switchboard operator reported to me that Jerry was reporting a bloody mess to the police," Partridge said. "I thought someone might be hurt."

"Come in, Doc," Chambrun called out.

"You'd better all come in," I said. "Jerry said the police will have questions for all of you."

There were expressions of shock and surprise, although the maid who had made the first discovery must have told them what to expect. I have to concede that the wreckage here in the living room and the bloody mess in the bedroom and bathroom would have been hard to take without feeling surprise and shock, no matter how thoroughly you'd been warned of what to expect.

"The blood is in the next room, I take it," Doc Partridge said. He walked on through to join Herzog and Jerry.

"The police are going to be asking if anyone saw Toby March leave this suite. Man in a black mask."

"When is he supposed to have left?" Mrs. Kniffin, the housekeeper, asked. "Last night? This morning?"

"He was performing in the Blue Lagoon till about one-thirty this morning," Chambrun said. "When he came up here to his suite, I don't know."

One of the men who wandered in with Mrs. Kniffin and

her maids spoke up. I recognized him as one of the musicians in Toby March's group. "I'm Ben Lewis," he said. "Guitar and also piano when Toby isn't playing it himself. Frankie Pasqua can answer most of your questions. He always knows where Toby is."

"Maybe not today," Chambrun said, his mouth a thin, tight line even when he spoke. "He doesn't answer his own phone. Someone suggested a lady."

Ben Lewis, dark-skinned and tired-looking, shrugged. "Saturday nights, I suppose, yes. He didn't have to report to Toby until the next business day, which would be tomorrow."

"You know who his girlfriend is?" Chambrun asked.

Lewis grinned. "Better make that plural, Mr. Chambrun. Girlfriends."

"Can you start us off with one?"

"A name, an address—no," Lewis said. "There's the red-haired one with the beautiful boobs. Frankie calls her Maggie. But Maggie who and an address, never. People have given up last names in this day and age. There's the black-haired gal with the searchlight smile. He calls her Sue, but Sue Who is a mystery. This was his first night here, so Frankie probably hasn't had much chance to sweep any of your locals into his net."

" 'Business manager,' he was called," Chambrun said. "I know he made the deal with Mark for the engagement here. What about the last date you played? Would he have had a chance there to sweep some gals into his net? Would that be a place to look for him?"

"Atlanta, Georgia? Not likely he took off for there after we

11

shut up shop last night. Frankie was here when we played our last number last night—this morning."

"No one could have lost that much blood and walked out of here without help," Lieutenant Herzog said from the bedroom doorway. "Pints of it."

"The body only holds a few pints," Doc Partridge said. "If the blood in there all came from one person, he hasn't got long to live."

"Does Toby March have a doctor?" Chambrun asked. "That doctor would know what March's blood type is. We'd know then whether he was the victim."

"Not for sure," the doctor said. "March's blood type could be type O, negative. If the lab shows that's the type in there, you'd be able to guess. It's not like fingerprints, which can give you a positive identification. Thousands and thousands of people have type O, negative blood. No way to determine that the blood in there is any particular person's. If you can find out what March's blood type is, the best you can do is make an educated guess that the person who bled in the bedroom could have been March, if his blood type matches. You can't be sure it was March. It could be type A or B, which are just as common."

"You know who March's doctor is?" Chambrun asked Ben Lewis.

"No. Toby was apparently healthy as a horse. Never even had a cold in the time I've worked for him."

"Which is how long?" Lieutenant Herzog asked.

"About four years," Lewis said.

"Then you can tell us what he looks like," Herzog said. "We can send out a general alarm on him."

"Would you believe that in all the time I've worked for him, I've never seen him without his black mask?"

"Sounds unreal," Herzog said.

"The story I got when I came to work for Toby came from Frank Pasqua," Lewis said. "Toby was a third-rate pianist playing with an unheard-of group in London. No reputation. No publicity. One day, someone tossed a bomb into a bus he was riding in to work. The explosion blew away his face. It looked like a raw hamburger, sprinkled with A-1 sauce, Frankie told me. Plastic surgery didn't work. He couldn't appear in public without shocking everyone who saw him. He had to hide out. That's when he developed the act he does now, recreating the music of famous stars. He has to stay behind the black mask. It wouldn't work if he exposed his disfigurement. I don't even know what his name was before he went into hiding behind that mask."

"There must be a police record of the bombing," Herzog said. "It would have the names of the people who were hurt. March's name, whatever it was then, would appear in that record." The detective looked around the room. "It's hard to believe no one heard this place being smashed up."

"Soundproof," Chambrun said.

"I still have to think March is the person who was hurt here," Herzog said. "He was doing his act in the Blue Lagoon until one-thirty in the morning. When that was finished, he'd have come back to this room, wouldn't he? If he found it the way it is now, he'd have called hotel security, wouldn't he? Of course he would. So it happened after he got here. He couldn't call because he was seriously hurt. I don't think there's any doubt that Toby March was beaten, badly hurt, and then taken away somewhere by the attacker. This guy Pasqua can probably tell us who had it in for him. Our first job is to find Pasqua."

"Unless Frankie hears about this on the radio or sees it on television," Ben Lewis said, "there's no reason for him to show up here till tomorrow morning. That's when he's supposed to connect up with Toby."

Chambrun looked at me. "Turn everyone loose on finding Pasqua, Mark," he said.

"You'd better notify the radio and TV people," Herzog said. "That way Pasqua may come to us, find himself for us."

My connections with the media were pretty good, and by three o'clock that afternoon radios all over the country were blaring out the news of the ugliness at the Beaumont. An hour later, there were interviews with Toby March's musicians, with famous people whose music he had "recreated," and with producers, like Chambrun, who had booked March's act and profited from it. Our switchboard was flooded with calls from reporters who wanted to corner Chambrun. My boss was almost as famous as Toby March himself. Being able to link them together was news with a capital N.

The thing we'd hoped for—a contact from Frankie Pasqua, Toby March's manager and perhaps closest friend—didn't happen. It was irritating but not unreasonable. If Pasqua was involved with a beautiful woman somewhere, he wouldn't reasonably be listening to the radio or TV.

There was an aspect of that late afternoon's doings that I hadn't anticipated. There were literally hundreds of phone calls, both to the Beaumont and, I learned later, to police headquarters from people who claimed to have seen a man in a black mask wandering the city streets. You would have to believe that a substantial segment of our male population was wandering around the city masked.

"The passion to get into the spotlight," Chambrun said, when I expressed my astonishment. "And this is a beaut! You don't have to give an exact description, just the black mask. It will waste hours and hours of skilled police time, because the police will have to follow up on these calls until they recognize that seeing men in black masks is an epidemic disease."

We did, along about suppertime, get a totally unexpected offer of help. A phone call came to me in my office.

"You don't know me, Mr. Haskell," a pleasant woman's voice said. "My name is Millicent Huber. I am an old friend of Toby March's. I'm here in the hotel with another friend of Toby's. We thought we might be helpful. Could we come and talk with you?"

"Of course," I said. "Ask any hotel employee, and they will show you where my office is."

"On our way," the lady said.

I don't know what I expected, but Miss Millicent Huber and the gentleman with her were, for some reason, not it. Miss Huber was a handsome middle-aged woman, and by middle-aged I mean early forties. Her companion was a man older than she, with short-cut white hair and a military bearing. He was introduced as Colonel Archibald Watson.

"Arch and I probably know Toby March better than anyone else," Miss Huber said.

Watson's handshake was firm. "I can't say that meeting you

is a pleasure, Mr. Haskell," Watson said, "not under the circumstances." He sounded very British.

"Arch is a kind of policeman," Millicent Huber said.

"Her Majesty's military intelligence," Watson said.

"Her Majesty?"

"The Queen of England, of course," Watson said.

"We both met Toby in England not long after his terrible accident," Miss Huber said. "He went to a London hospital for plastic surgery by a famous British surgeon. I was a nurse in the hospital and Arch was an orderly."

"You two didn't get here from London because of what's been on radio," I said. "There hasn't been time."

"We were here last night for Toby's opening in the Blue Lagoon," Millicent Huber said.

"You came here from London for that?"

"Toby thought it was the high point in his career so far. He wanted us to share it with him," Millicent Huber said.

"Have you seen him since last night's show?"

"We saw him after the show—in the Blue Lagoon, along with an army of fans. There was no way to be private with him, so we made a date to have dinner with him tonight."

"How bad is the situation they describe on the radio?" Watson asked me.

I described the wrecked living room, the bloody bedroom.

"I don't like the sound of it," Watson said.

"Do you know anyone who might have had it in for Toby March?" I asked him.

"There is no one!" Millicent Huber said. "Arch and I are probably his only close friends."

"There's Pasqua, his manager," Watson said. "Have you talked to him?"

I explained that Pasqua hadn't showed up yet. "The other musicians say that Pasqua turns to women on Saturday and Sunday nights. None of them know who it might have been last night. Unless he's heard the radio or seen the TV news, we may not hear from him until tomorrow morning. You say you were in on March's act early on?"

"From the very start," Millicent Huber said.

"You know what's behind that black mask of his?"

Watson nodded. "You'd never forget it if you saw it."

"But to get back to the start of Toby's act," Millicent said.

"The only thing that mattered to Toby after his disaster was his music," Watson said. "The hospital people moved a small spinet piano into the recreation room. Toby played a lot. He was awfully good with popular music. Nothing classical. Toby would stay in, plugging away at his music. One afternoon, when I came on duty, he seemed excited. 'Close your eyes and tell me who you hear,' he said to me. I closed my eyes and he began to play and sing—a tune I'll never forget: 'You Must Have Been a Beautiful Baby.' He stopped. 'Who were you listening to?' he asked me. Without any hesitation, I told him. 'Perry Como.' He let out a little screech of delight. That was the beginning. He had worked out a reason for hiding his mutilated face and still be able to perform in public. It was a stroke of genius. When he was released from a convalescent hospital, his face still scarred, he began playing in English music halls with his new act and became a sensational success. He perfected imitations of dozens of famous popular stars."

" 'Re-creations,' he called them, not imitations," Millicent Huber said.

17

"We think he came up here after the show was over in the Blue Lagoon," Lieutenant Herzog said. "Let himself in and found someone ransacking the joint."

"You're talking about Toby?" Watson asked.

"Who else?"

"Miss Huber and I were the last people to spend time with him downstairs before he decided to turn in," Watson said. "That was at about three-thirty."

"So you and Miss Huber were close to him?"

"Have been for years," Watson said.

The lady looked embarrassed. "I have been the—the woman in Toby's life for a long time," she said.

"Then you would know who his enemies are," Herzog said.

"I—I don't know of any," Millicent said.

"Why do you think it was any more than a common thief?" Watson asked. "A wealthy and famous performer is an obvious target for a hotel thief. Toby caught him red-handed, fought with him."

"And then?" Chambrun asked, speaking for the first time.

"If Toby won, that's the thief's blood in the next room," Watson said. "If the thief won, it's probably Toby's."

"So whoever won takes off," Chambrun said. "And takes the wounded man with him. Why? March would have called for help from us. Your thief would have just taken off. It's more complicated, Colonel, than just a thief caught going through the bureau drawers or the desk. Can you suggest why they're both gone?"

"Assuming that one of them was Toby, it does get complicated," Watson said. "Maybe Toby never came here. Maybe what happened here had nothing to do with him."

"So where did he go after he left the Blue Lagoon when he was headed for bed?" Chambrun asked.

"This is where he was staying," Millicent said. "Where else would he go? He didn't have any other living quarters here in New York. He's a legal resident of England."

"Was there anything he said to you at any time that suggested he expected any kind of trouble?"

"No," Millicent said.

"Who anticipates finding a thief in his rooms?" Watson asked.

"I still ask," Chambrun said, "why a thief would take a wounded Toby March out of here after the fight? And why would March take a strange thief somewhere?"

"The thief escaped after the fight and Toby chased after him," Watson said.

"You should take a look at the blood in the next room, Colonel," Chambrun said. "Whoever 'chased someone out of here,' as you suggest, there would have to be a trail. There isn't a sign of blood anywhere but in the bedroom."

No one had an answer.

"What kind of valuables would Toby have with him on a concert tour, Miss Huber?" Herzog asked.

"He had expensive studs and cuff links for his evening clothes," the woman said. "He always carried a lot of ready cash. Three or four hundred pounds in London, I suppose a thousand dollars here in America."

"He'd have been wearing the studs and cuff links, carrying all that cash. If those were what the thief was after, he'd have to come face-to-face with March. His best chance would be to wait for him here in his rooms."

"How did he get in?" Chambrun asked. "The door wasn't forced."

"Passkey?" Herzog suggested. "That's how the maid got in here and discovered this mess."

"Mrs. Kniffin?" Chambrun turned to the gray-haired housekeeper, who was standing in the corner of the room with Irma, the maid.

"I don't always have the passkey in my possession," Mrs. Kniffin said. "But I know who has it and for what purpose. No one would have it after midnight—in the early hours of the morning."

"Suppose a guest loses his key, how does he get in?" Herzog asked.

"There's a spare key locker at the front desk," Chambrun said.

"So that's where the thief got what he wanted," Herzog said.

"No way," Chambrun said. "The clerk wouldn't turn over the spare to just anyone. The thief couldn't steal it. The clerk wouldn't let him, and there are security people right there in the lobby."

"So March left the door unlocked when he went down to work in the Blue Lagoon."

"It's a Yale-type lock," Chambrun said. "All he'd have to do is close the door, and it's locked. The spare key, passkey theory doesn't work," Chambrun said.

"So come up with an answer," Herzog said.

"I don't have an answer," Chambrun said. "Unless the second person was a friend of March's, let in by March or given March's key by March."

"Are you suggesting March set himself up?" Herzog asked.

"Friend turned out not to be a friend," Chambrun said.

"Can you guess, Miss Huber, to whom March might have given his key?" Herzog asked.

"Me," Millicent said, "but he didn't."

"You, Colonel Watson?"

"But he didn't," Watson said.

"You're missing the one person who might have all the answers for you," Millicent Huber said. "Frank Pasqua, Toby's business manager. He's closer to Toby than a Siamese twin. Frankie isn't just a business manager, he is Toby's only close and trusted friend."

"According to one of the musicians I talked with," I said, "Pasqua's habit would be to be womanizing somewhere after the Saturday-night performance."

Millicent Huber smiled. "That's a pretty good guess, I'd say. And his date wouldn't be till late, after Toby's performance was over."

"March did his last number at about one-thirty this morning. Pasqua was there, standing at the bar. I saw him."

"No way he would be unavailable if Toby wanted him," Millicent said.

"Mark, circulate among the musicians," Chambrun said to me. "See if one of them can't give you a name of Pasqua's current girlfriend. Something a little more specific than what Ben Lewis gave you—'Maggie, the red-haired one with the beautiful boobs!' We need an address, a phone number."

It turned out to be easier than I'd expected. In the hall outside, reporters and March's musicians were gathered, along with a few curious sensation-seekers, and a couple of Jerry

Dodd's men, who were trying to keep things from getting out of hand.

Standing next to Ben Lewis was a girl with bright-red hair and bosoms about as sensational as I can ever remember seeing. Lewis introduced me to Maggie Hanson.

"She's here looking for Frankie," Ben said. "He's not in there?"

"No, and I'm supposed to be looking for the girl he might be dating. Not you, Miss Hanson?"

"I was supposed to be," the girl said. She had a husky, sexy voice. Pasqua certainly knew how to pick them. "Frankie was supposed to come to my place after the show was over. He never came."

"No phone call?"

"No. And that isn't like him. I gave up on him about daylight, a little angry that I'd been left out to dry. Then, this afternoon I heard on the radio about what had been found here."

"Cop inside would like to talk to you," I said.

"I can't tell him any more than I've told you," Maggie said. "But what can I lose?"

The security men let us back into March's suite. Ben Lewis came along with us. I saw the look of shock on the girl's face as she looked around the shattered room and heard her murmur, "Oh, wow!" I brought Herzog and Chambrun up to date.

"Broken dates not a habit of Pasqua's?" Herzog asked.

"No."

"You're his girlfriend?"

"Not in the way I think you mean it," Maggie said. "I'd have to say I was one of his girlfriends."

"So he could have ditched you to go out with someone else?"

"He could have," Maggie said. "But not without letting me know."

"Not a very satisfactory relationship," Herzog said.

"I guess you'd have to say it depends on what you wanted from a relationship," Maggie said. "If Frankie was an every-day thing in my life, I'd have to say it isn't very satisfactory."

"He's just a once-in-a-while guy in your life?"

"You could say that. The trouble is he's rarely here since he hooked up with Toby March. March is all over the world with his act, mostly in Europe. This date at the Beaumont is one of the rare times they've been in New York."

"But when they came here, you and Pasqua got together?"

"Yes." Maggie's smile was provocative. "When we get together, we have something very special going for us."

"But when he's somewhere else he's with some other woman. Right?"

"I can't expect him to be a monk, can I?"

"And are you a nun when he isn't here?" Herzog asked.

The girl gave him a cool smile. "What have these questions got to do with what's happened here?" she asked.

"We're trying to find out where to look for Pasqua. Wherever he is, he obviously hasn't heard the radio or seen the TV."

"If Frankie is with another girl," Maggie said, "you can be sure he isn't listening to the radio."

"He was here until March's show ended at one-thirty in the morning," Chambrun said, taking over. "Then he was sched-uled to go to you. He didn't, and he didn't let you know. You've explained that to yourself, Miss Hanson?"

23

"Yes, and another girl wasn't my explanation. Maybe that's vanity. But he's been so enthusiastic about our having time together, when he didn't come I knew it had to be March."

"How do you mean?"

"Toby March is Frankie's life, professionally and personally. If Toby had some kind of problem, Frankie would back him up, no matter who else got shut out. They aren't like a team—more like one person. Frankie loves the guy. When I heard on the radio what had been found here, I knew Frankie was in some kind of trouble."

"Did Pasqua ever tell you about any enemies March had?" Chambrun asked.

"He never told me anything about Toby's personal life," Maggie said. "He was like a priest or a doctor when it came to Toby's world. What he knew was confidential and secret."

"Do you know anyone with whom Pasqua might have shared those secrets?" Chambrun asked.

"No one, not some casual girlfriend, that's for sure," Maggie said. "Frankie and I were close but nothing unusual about Toby March ever came my way."

"Thanks for helping," Chambrun said.

"I wasn't much help, I'm afraid," Maggie said. "If you find Frankie, please let me know. I'm in the phone book."

"We're all pretty damn worried," Ben Lewis, the musician, said.

"You think of Toby March as being addicted to physical violence?" Chambrun asked.

"Last thing in the world," Lewis said. "I've never heard him raise his voice to anyone."

"You're forgetting one thing that will set Toby off like a rocket," Millicent Huber said.

"And that is?" Chambrun asked.

"A mask snatcher," Millicent said. "There's always some crazy fan around who wants to snatch off Toby's mask to see what it hides. That enrages Toby."

"You're suggesting some mask snatcher was waiting here for March?" Chambrun asked.

"I've been thinking along that line," Millicent said. "A photographer. Steps out of the next room and snaps a picture of Toby as he takes off the mask. Toby grabs the fireplace poker and tries to smash the camera. In the end he makes it, and wounds the photographer in the process. There's no picture left but there is a hurt man. Toby might take him somewhere for help. The photographer would go willingly."

"That's a very interesting guess, Miss Huber," Jerry Dodd said. "But that's all it is. A guess! We've been over this place from top to bottom and there isn't a sign anywhere of a smashed camera. And if Toby March wanted to get help for a man he'd injured, why did he sneak away? Why not call the hotel doctor, the hotel's hospital facilities, our emergency equipment?"

"He didn't know what was available," Millicent said.

"He's a world traveler," Jerry said. "He knows what a hotel like the Beaumont has available. Does he have a doctor of his own here in the city?"

"I think not."

"You are close enough to him to know—from what you've told us."

"He has a doctor in London. I don't think he's spent enough time in New York to have anything regular here."

"So what we need is evidence," Jerry said. "Evidence that

will back up elaborate guesses. Let's hope that Pasqua can come up with something when he shows."

"He's the closest person to Toby in this world," Ben Lewis said.

"I think that's true—except for me," Millicent Huber said.

2

Crime is not unheard-of in the Beaumont. As Chambrun has often said, the hotel is a "city within a city." It differs from any other small city you may know in one respect. The people who use it are transients; they are, by and large, strangers to each other. They have just one thing in common. They are rich. You don't stay at the Beaumont and enjoy its luxuries on the loose change in your pocket. Thus, the hotel guests are targets for criminal greed. Chambrun and Jerry Dodd and the entire staff are dedicated to making sure that our guests are not victimized by those criminals. But a bludgeoning with an iron poker is not the kind of thing they are on guard against.

A feeling of community does exist among the hundreds of people on the hotel staff. From the lowest shoeshine boy in the barbershop to the heads of special departments and facilities, everyone is held together by two things: loyalty to Chambrun, and pride in the efficient functioning of one of the greatest hotels anywhere.

"When one of my people lets me down," Chambrun says, "it will be time for me to quit. It would mean I'd been guilty of bad judgment when I hired that person."

In all the time I've worked for Chambrun, I've never known any one of his people to let him down. It didn't occur to me that Sunday evening that anything like this could have happened in Toby March's suite on the seventeenth floor.

There are two work shifts at the Beaumont—seven in the morning till seven at night, and seven at night till seven in the morning. There are some people who don't work that full night shift, and certain departments aren't functioning in the early hours of the morning—though it is a busy time in the hotel bars and nightclubs. But the people who had been working when Toby March left his friends, Colonel Watson and Millicent Huber, in the Blue Lagoon and went up to his suite to face whatever was waiting for him there, were not on duty now but were expected to return in about an hour. Chambrun gave me a list of key people to call at home. It couldn't be expected they were spending their time off listening to the radio and watching television. I found that most of the ones I reached hadn't been, and were shocked to hear what had happened. No one I talked to seemed to have seen or heard anything that seemed to be connected with a violence.

Between the calls I was making from my office, my phone rang.

"Haskell! What the hell is going on back there?"

I felt my hand tighten on the phone. I had spent a lot of time recently making the arrangements for Toby March's engagement in the Blue Lagoon. There was no mistaking this bouncy voice. My caller was Frankie Pasqua.

"Where the hell are you? The whole world has been looking for you!"

"I just switched on the television and heard a special report," Pasqua said.

"Why aren't you on your way here?"

There was something a little chilling about Pasqua's laughter. "I've got some unfinished business where I am," he said. It said "woman" loud and clear.

"You know your man has disappeared," I said.

"Don't worry about Toby," he said. "He can take care of himself, whatever the situation."

"You might wonder if you saw the shape his room was in and the gallons of blood spread around."

"I think you can count on it not being Toby's blood," Pasqua said.

"We've been wondering if it might be yours," I said.

"Well, it's not! You thought Toby and I had a fight? I make that man's world work for him, Haskell."

"The cops need you here," I said.

"After breakfast in the morning," he said. "If I could contribute anything I'd come. But right now—"

"Right now your girlfriend, Maggie, is here worrying about you."

"Tell her to cheer up," Pasqua said. "When I explain it to her in the morning, she'll understand. Just let the cops know I'm okay, and that I'm of no use to them as far as this case is concerned. Don't worry about Toby. He'll probably be back long before I am."

"When you show up here, Lieutenant Herzog will probably have a nice cell in the slammer waiting for you," I said.

"You're a missing piece in his puzzle, and you're deliberately holding out on him."

"I'll worry about that when the time comes," Pasqua said. He hung up on me.

Herzog nearly hit the ceiling when I got to him with my account of Pasqua's call to me. I found him in Chambrun's office along with Chambrun, Jerry Dodd, and Colonel Watson, who seemed to have been accepted as an ally by the others.

"Tomorrow morning after breakfast," Herzog fumed. "Who the hell does he think he is, obstructing justice?"

"He says he doesn't have anything to tell you," I said.

"I, goddamn it, have things to ask him!"

"Wasn't he at all concerned about Toby March, his boss?" Jerry Dodd asked.

"He said March could take care of himself."

"Against a man swinging an iron poker at him?" Herzog asked.

Chambrun broke his silence then, looking hard at me. "You have no doubt that it was Pasqua who talked to you, Mark?"

"No doubt," I said. "You remember I spent a good part of a week negotiating March's contract for the Blue Lagoon."

"What's so distinctive about his voice?" Herzog asked.

"It's not so much the sound of his voice," I said, "but a kind of bright, bouncy way of talking."

"That's quite true," Watson said. "It's a unique pattern, one you're not likely to forget when you hear it for a second time."

"I think we mustn't forget one thing," Chambrun said. "We are missing a man who makes a profession of imitating voices."

"Are you suggesting that what Haskell heard was Toby March imitating his friend?" Herzog asked.

"When you have a master imitator on the loose, it's something to consider, isn't it, Lieutenant?"

"But why?"

"That phone call was designed to do two things, wasn't it?" Chambrun asked. "It was to assure us that Frank Pasqua was alive and well and in no trouble, and that Toby March was competent enough to take care of himself and also isn't in trouble."

"We're supposed to think two cleaning women were fighting each other with an iron poker in 17C?" Jerry Dodd asked.

"Something like that," Chambrun said.

"Son of a bitch!" Herzog said.

"We just have to wonder," Chambrun said.

" 'Unfinished business.' Did he give you any idea what that might be?" Jerry asked me.

"I got the distinct impression he was talking about a woman," I said.

"What about that Maggie what's-her-name who is waiting around downstairs?"

"He said he would explain everything to her when he sees her—after breakfast tomorrow," I said.

"You honestly think he's going to turn up after breakfast tomorrow?" Herzog asked anyone who might answer.

"If it was Pasqua on the phone, maybe," Chambrun said. "If it was Toby March, I'd say never!" He turned to Watson. "How bad is Toby March's face? I've heard it described as 'raw meat.' "

"That's the way it was in the beginning," Watson said.

"Pretty horrible. But no one I know has seen his face since the operation in London."

"Then he could put on a hat, pull down the brim, and no one would give him a second look?" Chambrun asked.

"I suppose that's possible," Watson said.

"So he could have been coming and going here for the last day and nobody would notice him?" Chambrun asked.

"I'd say that could be happening," Watson said. "I'd like to say one thing, Mr. Chambrun. I think perhaps I'd better not be sitting in with this group. You've gotten yourselves worked up to believing that Toby March is the villain of this story. I've known him too long and too well to believe anything like that for an instant. I don't propose to lend you a hand in proving that my friend is some kind of violent monster."

"So help us prove that he isn't," Chambrun said.

"Let's wait till after breakfast tomorrow morning," Watson said. "When Pasqua shows up, we'll probably get some missing answers."

"If Pasqua shows up," Chambrun said. "God save me from a friend like him. I'm in deep trouble, and he has to solve his sex problems before offering me any help. I wouldn't need that kind of friend. And there's more to it than that."

"More?"

"Pasqua's financial security depends on Toby March's good health, doesn't it? Just for tomorrow's dollar, he wouldn't back away from helping Toby March in trouble."

"Let's go over what we know for certain," Jerry Dodd said. "Toby finished his performance in the Blue Lagoon about one-thirty this morning. When it was finished, he joined you, Colonel Watson, and Miss Huber at your table for a sort of family reunion."

"It wasn't much of a reunion," Watson said. "We were crushed by fans who wanted Toby's autograph. He was pretty exhausted from the night's doings and suggested we all retire and meet today when we were rested. He was to call us when he got moving later in the day. Of course, as you know, he never did."

"But he did go up to his room after he left you," Jerry said. "The night elevator operator remembers him. Why not? Man in a black mask. I had one of my security men on the seventeenth floor to help ward off rubbernecking fans. He saw Toby let himself into his rooms at about three-thirty."

"Where someone was waiting for him and the war started," Chambrun said.

"With a security man just outside the door?" Watson asked.

"The best soundproofing money can buy," Chambrun said.

"My security man had one other item to report," Jerry Dodd said. "Pasqua's room adjoined Toby's suite on seventeen. There is a connecting door between 17C and 17D. That was unlocked on orders from Toby March. He wanted Pasqua to have free access to his rooms. They're built that way so that 17C can be enlarged for a big family."

"So your man saw both Toby and Pasqua go into their rooms?" Watson asked.

"Pasqua at two-thirty, Toby an hour later."

"The important thing is, he never saw either of them leave," Chambrun said. "Until the maid discovered the wreckage in 17C, no one saw anyone come or go."

"Your man stayed on duty all that time?" Watson asked Jerry.

"No. Along about five o'clock, Toby's fans had stopped nosing around. My man was relieved and left the 17th floor."

"So there is a stretch of about eight hours in which no one had a special reason to watch the rooms on seventeen?" Watson asked.

"And in that time Toby March and Frank Pasqua have disappeared. The man who lost all that blood in 17C would have needed help to get out of there," Chambrun said. "Two men don't just walk away when one of them needs help without attracting attention. Unless they never left the hotel. The injured man, or dead man, whichever it is, could still be hidden somewhere in the hotel, Jerry. In the basement machinery areas, storerooms. The other man, who wasn't hurt, is long gone."

"We'll go over every inch of the place," Jerry said.

"The whole thing may explain itself when Pasqua calls you tomorrow morning," Watson said.

"If he calls," Chambrun said, "and if we haven't found his body hidden in one of the basement storerooms."

3

My assignment was to stay by my phone in case Pasqua or whoever was faking him should call. The hotel switchboard was alerted to be ready to trace any call that came my way. I waited in my office, and when the phone rang it wasn't from the outside. Jerry Dodd was calling from somewhere in the basement area.

"We've found something down here, Mark," he said. "A dead man."

"Oh, brother!"

"It isn't Pasqua and it isn't Toby March," Jerry said. "No identification on him, and so far no one has been able to identify him. The boss wants you to have a look. You just might—"

"How was he killed?" I asked. "I assume he didn't die a natural death."

"Skull beaten in," Jerry said.

"The poker in 17C?"

"Possible. Possibly not. Coincidence if it was. Basement Two, north end, Mark. Step on it."

The whole hotel army was congregated at the north end of Basement Two—Chambrun, Jerry, Doc Partridge, Lieutenant Herzog, and Larry Short, the security man who had been stationed on seventeen. The body was stretched out on a tool bench against the far wall.

"Happy if you can tell us who this character is, Haskell," the police lieutenant said.

It might be easy for you to say, "Yes, I've seen this man before" or "No, I've never seen him before." But my life is made up of daily encounters with hundreds of people moving through the hotel lobby and in the service departments. Unless I have personal contact with someone, I am surrounded by a blur of faces I have no reason to recall.

This man was tall, dark-skinned—not black. I guessed Spanish, perhaps South American. The left side of his forehead and the hair on the left side of his head were matted with blood. He had on an expensive, well-tailored suit. That didn't suggest a tradesman who might have business in the basement.

"No dice," I told Lieutenant Herzog.

"You're sure?"

"I'm sure I don't remember if I ever saw him."

"No wallet or any identification," Herzog said. "But the wounds that killed him are the kind that could have been made by that poker up in 17C."

"But I don't think this man bled enough to account for all the blood we found up there," Doc Partridge said.

"There are dozens of tools down here in the basement that

could have inflicted his wounds," Chambrun said. "We'll keep looking."

"I say his wounds were inflicted in Toby March's suite and he was brought down here later," Herzog said. "After the security man went off duty."

"But how did he get into March's rooms?" Chambrun asked.

"Not while I was on duty," Larry Short said. "I went on about midnight. Not after that. He didn't go in with Pasqua when he came up at two-thirty. He didn't go in with March an hour later. He wasn't among the people I hassled with who were after autographs."

At that moment, another one of Jerry Dodd's men guided Watson and Millicent Huber down the basement corridor. Millicent Huber was hanging on to Watson's arm as if her life depended on it.

"Sorry to put you through this, Miss Huber," Chambrun said.

Watson disengaged himself from Millicent's clutch and went straight over to the bench where the murdered man was stretched out. He looked down at the man for a long time, bent down to look more closely.

"I don't remember ever seeing him before," he said finally. He held out his hand to Millicent. She took it and moved reluctantly toward the body. She let out a little gasp when she saw the bloodied head.

"No! No, I've never seen him before," she said.

"I take it you think this is connected with what happened upstairs," Watson said.

"Be something of a coincidence if it isn't, wouldn't you say?" Chambrun answered.

"Of course, until they do an autopsy on this man," Doc Partridge said, "we won't know if he lost enough blood to account for what was found upstairs."

"If he was just left to bleed?" Herzog asked.

"If he was killed instantly, he wouldn't go on bleeding and bleeding," Doc Partridge said. "No heart action to pump it out!"

"I had high hopes for you and Miss Huber, Colonel," Chambrun said. "The dead man's coloring suggests a Mediterranean country. Since most of March's early career was European, and you and Miss Huber were part of his life in those days, I had high hopes this man would be an old acquaintance of yours."

"Not this one," Watson said.

Chambrun turned to the woman, who was still trembling like a leaf. "If Toby would confide in anyone, it would be you, Miss Huber. Has he ever mentioned an enemy who might have threatened him, or whom he feared?"

"No! When I first met Toby I was a nurse in the hospital where he came for repairs to his brutally damaged face. We . . . we got to be friends. In time, that led to intimate conversations about our lives, our families, and eventually the business world into which he found himself launched. I never heard Toby mention an enemy whom he feared or distrusted."

"Frank Pasqua?"

"Most trusted of everyone," Millicent said.

"The only people who might know of some kind of feuding in the music business are the musicians," Watson said. "Ben Lewis, Sam Callahan, Dan Potter, Dave Morton.

They're all here in the hotel. If the dead man is someone in the music world, one of those boys might know him."

"Get them down here," Herzog ordered Jerry Dodd.

"It probably is just a coincidence," Watson said. "Not connected with what went on upstairs."

Chambrun gave him a twisted little smile. "You go to your church and I'll go to mine," he said.

Jerry Dodd's people produced the four young men who were the musicians for Toby March's extraordinary act. They had been told why they were wanted. They stared curiously at the dead man and then at each other. It was obvious they didn't know the man by sight.

"None of us knows this guy," Ben Lewis said. He was the one I'd met. Sunday was their day off, and they were casually dressed — gaudy sport shirts, blue jeans, sneakers. It was almost like a uniform.

"Could he be some kind of fan of March's whom you might have seen in your audience?" Chambrun asked.

"We can't see anyone in the audience," Lewis said. "The stage lights are so bright and focused directly on us, we can't even see anyone in the front row."

"I'd appreciate it if you four boys and Colonel Watson and Miss Huber would come up to my office," Chambrun said. "I'd like to talk to those of you who've had an everyday life with March and Pasqua."

"Let me remind you, Mr. Chambrun," Lieutenant Herzog said, "that I am officially investigating this case."

"Let me remind you, Lieutenant," Chambrun said, "that

what has happened here was in my hotel and the people it has happened to were working for me."

"The dead man wasn't working for you!"

"But he was almost certainly killed by someone who was," Chambrun said, his voice as cold as a winter wind.

"The murderer could be just a common hotel thief who managed to get into March's suite."

"Then one of these people may be able to tell me what's missing," Chambrun said, motioning us to follow him to the elevator.

When we got upstairs, I could tell that someone had come into the office behind me. I turned. It was Jerry Dodd.

"I've got one for you, boss," Jerry said. "Registered in 1503 is a couple—Colonel and Mrs. Archibald Watson."

"Colonel and *Mrs.* Watson?"

"What's interesting about it is," Jerry went on, "that Mrs. Watson turns out to be Millicent Huber, who is supposed to be Toby March's lady."

"My God!"

At that moment, as if on cue, Watson, the lady we'd just been discussing, and the four young musicians crowded through the office door.

"You wanted to talk to us?" Watson said in his clipped, British voice.

"You are full of surprises," Chambrun said, "especially you, Mrs. Watson."

The woman lowered her head, moving it from side to side. "You know?" she asked in an unsteady voice.

"Not much fails to drift my way in this hotel," Chambrun said, "except the identity of that dead man in the basement. You still say he couldn't possibly be Toby March?"

"No way," Millicent said.

"The phony registration was Toby's idea," Watson said.

"It was his idea that you should be living with his lady?" Chambrun asked.

"Just a front," Watson said. "I'm actually staying at the University Club, a couple of blocks down the avenue."

"If I stayed close to Toby," Millicent Huber said, "I'd be swarmed by people wanting me to point out Toby. His business, his career, depend on people not being able to identify him."

"It occurred to me," Jerry Dodd broke in, "the man down in the basement might be a fan. One of you young fellows might recognize him from the audience."

"We told Mr. Chambrun earlier that we can't see the audience," Ben Lewis said. "The stage lights are focused directly on us. I couldn't recognize my own mother in the first row!"

"Can you draw me a sketch of how March looks?" Chambrun asked Millicent.

"I've made Toby a solemn promise never to do that for anyone. His career could depend on it," she replied.

"His career may depend on our being able to locate him now," Jerry Dodd said.

"You had better, all of you, look at the alternatives in this case," Chambrun said. "Two-thirty in the morning, Frank Pasqua goes into his room, which joins March's. At three-thirty, March goes into his room. Neither man has been seen again, but there was violence in which someone had nearly bled to death. March or Pasqua? Not the man in the basement. He didn't bleed enough, according to Doc Partridge, to account for what we found in 17C. So March or Pasqua.

Why would either man take the other man away without asking for help that was right at the other end of a phone line in the room?"

"Did either March or Pasqua have a personal doctor somewhere in New York?" Jerry Dodd asked.

"I don't know of any doctor," Millicent Huber said. "Certainly Toby didn't have one."

"So if Pasqua had one, why would he call in about 'unfinished business' that suggested a girl?" Chambrun asked. "He should have been deeply concerned if March was the person who was wounded. That phone call has to have been a phony."

"And you think Toby made it, faking Pasqua's voice?" Watson asked.

"Who else?"

"That theory is pure guesswork," Watson said.

"So give me a more intelligent guess," Chambrun said. "There isn't a reason I can see for anyone but March making that fake call."

"Only you think it was faked," Watson said.

"And you think Pasqua would leave his boss, his bread-and-butter, seriously hurt while he kept a date with a girl?"

"He didn't take what he heard on the radio seriously."

"Why not?"

"Because he left him in 17C alive and well."

"Your way, nothing makes sense," Chambrun said. "March was the last person seen by Jerry's man going into the suite on seventeen. Pasqua was already there."

"In his room."

"But able to walk into March's room without showing himself to the security man."

"And there he finds the dead man in the basement, not yet dead. He knows who he is, or just takes it for granted he is a hotel thief, or a greedy fan of March's. They fight, and Pasqua slugs the man with the fireplace poker, fatally. He waits for March to show up so they can decide together what to do with the corpse."

"If the dead man is dead then."

"If he is, they must decide how to dispose of him."

"If he isn't and is just being held prisoner by Pasqua, what happens then?"

Watson shook his head slowly. "So, the stranger gets possession of the weapon and severely beats one of the other two, causing the possibly fatal bleeding."

"Pasqua or March?"

"Has to be one of them."

"So why does the one who is left take the wounded man away from the hotel?"

"Because you haven't found him doesn't mean he isn't somewhere here in the hotel," Watson said.

"We'll find him if he is," Jerry Dodd said. "We'll go through every room in the place, guests or not."

"They didn't park the dead man in one of the guest's rooms," Watson said.

"And who killed him?"

"March or Pasqua in a second fight," Jerry suggested.

"And why hide him?" Chambrun asked. "Why not call security?"

"When you have the answer to that, you've got the case solved," Watson said.

Chambrun turned to Jerry. "Get every inch of this place searched," he said. "I'll be up in my penthouse."

"Giving up?" Watson asked.

"Like most of us, I need a breather," Chambrun said. "The press and media people aren't going to ease up."

There are three penthouses on the roof. Chambrun occupies one. The second one is kept ready for special and important guests. The third one is occupied and owned by a very special old lady, Victoria Haven. She has owned it since the days before Chambrun and his people bought the Beaumont. She was allowed to stay on and is certainly one of Chambrun's cherished friends.

There was another reason for Chambrun's rather abrupt leaving of the scene. There was a lady waiting for him up in his penthouse; Betsy Ruysdale, his fabulous secretary. She has golden-blond hair, a sexy figure, and a marvelous sense of humor that makes her the only one able to get Chambrun to smile and laugh, a talent none of the rest of us has.

At his desk, Chambrun dialed four numbers — an in-house call.

"Sorry I left you hanging out to dry," he said when someone answered. It had to be Betsy. "If you have been listening to the radio or watching the tube, you'll know why. Well, I'll bring you up to date in a few minutes."

The colonel, Millicent Huber, and the four musicians had no idea to whom he was talking.

"I'll be back presently," Chambrun said to them.

I knew later from Betsy what happened next. Chambrun went up to the penthouse where she had been waiting for him. She hadn't been watching or listening to the news, so he told her what they had found in 17C; the bloody disappearance of both Toby March and Frank Pasqua without any call for help; the dead stranger in the basement. While he was still telling it all to her, the phone rang. He was tempted not to answer. He wanted just a little time free of the mess. But the phone rang and rang. He answered.

"Victoria!" he said.

It was the octogenarian lady who lived in the penthouse across the roof from him. Victoria Haven's unsteady voice was shakier than usual.

"I know what's been going on, Pierre. The radio. How horrible!"

"Pretty ugly," he said.

"But that isn't why I've called. There's a man out on the roof snooping around your penthouse, trying to look in the windows."

"You recognize him?"

"No, but you know my eyesight."

"The woods are full of crazies tonight," Chambrun said. "Thanks for calling."

He explained to Betsy and walked out onto the roof through a side door. She heard him call out, "Hey, you!"

And then there were two sharp explosions. They sounded like what she imagined were gunshots. She ran to the door and called out, "Pierre, Pierre!"

The phone rang. It was Victoria Haven again. "My God, what happened, Betsy? It sounded like shots. Pierre is lying face down outside your dining-room windows."

Betsy ran out onto the roof. Chambrun was where Victoria had said he was, face down under the dining-room windows, motionless.

"Pierre!"

45

Betsy knelt beside him, touched his face. Her hand came away bloody. Old Mrs. Haven was stumbling across the roof toward her.

"He's hurt!" Betsy called out. "Call Dr. Partridge, Victoria. Tell him Pierre's been shot. It's an emergency."

She felt frantically for a pulse at his wrists. Either there was none, or she was being clumsy in her panic.

The wound was in the side of his head, at his left temple. She took a handkerchief out of her pocket and tried to stop the bleeding with it. She felt herself shaking from head to foot. It was more serious than anything she could handle. There was no response of any kind when she spoke his name. Not even the twitch of an eyelid.

Part Two

1

Dr. Partridge arrived with two bellhops carrying an emergency stretcher.

"Oh, my God!" he said, after his first quick examination.

"Is he—?" Betsy asked.

"He's alive," the doctor said, "but we've got to get him to the hospital in a hurry. It's a very near thing, Betsy. Who shot him?"

"I have no way of knowing. Mrs. Haven saw someone snooping around out on the roof and warned Pierre. He went out on the roof to scare the person off. Then there were two shots."

"Both of them hit him. It will be a miracle if—"

They loaded Chambrun onto the stretcher and hurried off with him. Mrs. Haven was standing by, clinging desperately to Betsy.

"I—I sent him out there. I never dreamed—"

"Of course you didn't."

I got back into the situation live a little after that. When

Chambrun had headed for his penthouse, I'd gone to my own office, which adjoins his, leaving Watson, Millicent Huber, and the four musicians to fend for themselves. There would be nationwide publicity to deal with presently, and there still was not a satisfactory story to tell about the disappearance of Toby March and Frank Pasqua, and the dead man in the basement. I was working on it when Betsy Ruysdale got me on the phone with the grim news about Chambrun.

In a state of shock, I headed for Dr. Partridge's office. He was there, looking a little shaken himself.

"They've taken Pierre to St. Mark's hospital," he told me. "Dr. Horace Lockwood, the best brain specialist in the city, is taking care of him."

"And—?"

"Nothing positive yet, Mark. You may think it's good news if I tell you I'd guess Pierre's chances were about fifty-fifty. I don't feel optimistic."

"I'm going over to St. Mark's to see him," I said.

"Not much point. If he comes to, he wouldn't recognize you or speak to you. It will be a miracle if he ever gets back to anything like normal."

"He'd expect me to stand behind him," I said. "Just on the chance he might know I was there—"

"As far as I know," the doctor said, "there's no lead of any kind to the person who shot him. If someone else had been shot, searching for that gunman is what Chambrun would be doing, not holding hands with the victim."

"I'm not Chambrun," I said.

"You're part of him," the doctor said. "Betsy is part of him,

Jerry Dodd is part of him, the whole damned staff is part of him. Put yourselves together and you've got the same talents working for you. Don't stall, Mark. You have a would-be killer to catch."

He was right, of course. We should all be huddled together working out a plan of action. I headed upstairs for the penthouses. Jerry Dodd was already there with old Mrs. Haven. He hadn't needed anyone to tell him where to go.

"I feel guilty, terribly guilty," Mrs. Haven said, for my benefit. "I told Pierre there was someone out there instead of calling Jerry. I should have known Pierre would try to handle things himself."

"But you saw the man who shot him," I said.

"Not really," Mrs. Haven said. "My eyesight is too poor."

"Medium height," Jerry said. "Wearing a snap-brim hat which would have hidden his face."

"You saw the shooting?" I asked the old lady.

She nodded, her mouth muscles twitching. "I saw Pierre come out, move around toward the rear of the penthouse. Then there were two bright flashes and I knew—I knew. I saw Pierre go down—"

"And the man?"

"He came out from behind the penthouse and ran for the elevators."

"Nothing memorable about him?"

"Very quick, very agile."

"But if you saw him down in the lobby or out on the street, you couldn't finger him?" Jerry asked.

"I'm afraid not, Jerry. He was just a shadow."

Jerry made an impatient gesture. "We seem to be caught

up in a crazy game," he said. "We're looking for a popular musician who wouldn't be recognized if he walked out on the Palace Theater stage. We're looking for an assassin who could step up beside us at a bar and not be recognized, though he was seen. We've got a dead man on our hands who gives us no clue to who he is or where he comes from."

"You connected all three things?" I asked.

Jerry gave me a sour look. "We have a murder, an attempted murder, and a disappearance that involved much violence and that could mean another murder. All almost within shouting distance of each other, all in the space of an hour and a half or so. Are you innocent-minded enough to assume they have no connection?"

"I guess that would be hard to swallow."

"Bet on it," Jerry said. "I'd like to get Betsy to have a look at that guy in the basement. She may be able to connect him to Chambrun."

"When Chambrun couldn't himself?"

"All kinds of crackpots try to get to him, and it's Betsy's job to keep them out," Jerry said. "That guy might ring a bell with her."

"You can be sure she followed Chambrun's ambulance to the hospital."

"That figures. Well, the guy in the basement isn't going anywhere. When she gets back, tell Betsy I need to see her."

"Will do."

Sleep never crossed my mind as a necessity. My thoughts, my emotions were all at the hospital where Chambrun was, I hoped, fighting for survival. Downstairs outside my office, it appeared that half the press corps in the United States was waiting for some kind of answer from me, first as to what had happened to Toby March, and second, how was Chambrun doing. I had no positive information on either score. Chambrun had still been alive ten minutes ago. March and Frank Pasqua had disappeared into limbo, without a clue as to where that limbo might be.

There was a red-haired girl among the reporters who was trying to edge her way toward me. Maggie Hanson. Her face was the color of a white china plate. It wasn't reportorial curiosity but fear of some sort that produced that pallor. She finally got close enough to me to speak.

"I need to talk to you, Mr. Haskell," she said.

"Join the army," I said, gesturing to the crowd around us.

"In private," she said. "My name is Margaret Hanson, Frank Pasqua's girlfriend."

"Try that door over there and wait inside for me," I said.

I made a brief speech to the reporters. There was no explanation as to what had happened to March and Pasqua. No one could identify the man who had shot Chambrun, who was just hanging on by a hair. When I had anything, I'd pass it on to them. Then I followed the Hanson girl into my office.

She was sitting at my desk, clinging to the arms of my desk chair. Her whole body was shaking.

"There's nothing I can tell you," I said. "I had a phone call I thought was Pasqua, but some doubt has been thrown on that."

"What kind of doubt? Didn't he identify himself?"

"Yes. And I'd had dealings with him. I thought I recognized his voice without any question. He said he'd heard on the radio or TV what had happened here. But he was certain Toby March could take care of himself. He had 'unfinished business' to take care of."

"What kind of unfinished business?"

"He was laughing when he said it. I thought he was talking about a girl."

"Never! Not in New York. Here I'm the only girl in his life."

"Did he have a date with you he hadn't kept?"

"Yes and no," the girl said. "He has a date with me every night he's in New York. But on an opening night, with a specially curious crowd present, he stays with Toby until it's completely over."

"But he didn't stay with him last night," I said. "He went up to the seventeenth floor at two-thirty. Our security man saw him. Toby March didn't go up until an hour later. He was also seen by security."

"None of it makes any sense," the girl said. "He would have called me if he wasn't coming—and he didn't. Hasn't. And why would he call you?"

"He knew me and that I would know exactly what was going on here. Chambrun thought March might have faked his voice on the phone to me. Possible?" I asked.

"Toby could imitate him so well I couldn't have told the difference myself," the girl said.

"Then the call could have been a fake—March for Pasqua," I said. "We were meant to believe Pasqua was safe when he wasn't."

"Frank has no reason to hide!"

"But March does?"

"Hiding is his life," the girl said. "Would you believe, I traveled around Europe with them for two seasons and I never saw Toby without his mask. I wouldn't know him if he walked into this room now without his mask. It was Frank's job to help him keep his identity hidden."

"So that's what he's doing? Keeping him out of sight?" I asked.

"If Toby was recognized, identified by the police, his whole ball game would be over. His career would be over. Frank would do anything to help Toby see to it that this doesn't happen."

"We have to believe one of them is badly hurt," I said.

"Frank would hide Toby," she said. "And Toby would hide Frank if Frank was hurt and might somehow expose him, by speaking his name or calling out to him."

"Is there some place one of them would take the other in a crisis like that?" I asked.

"If Toby has friends in this country, I don't know who they are. There's no one close to Frank that I know of. All their close contacts are in Europe."

"The dead man in the basement. He might be someone they know of from abroad. Would you mind having a look at him?"

"Anything that might help us find Frank," she said. "It's a very long shot, Mr. Haskell."

"Long shots are all we've got," I said.

The dead man in the basement was not without company. Herzog was there along with a fingerprint expert and a police photographer. They were getting ready to send out a request for help from police forces all around the country. I explained to Herzog why we were there.

He gestured to the body on the bench. "Be my guest!"

I led Margaret Hanson over and she stood for a minute, looking down. Then, suddenly, her hand closed over my wrist, so tightly I thought she would shut off the circulation.

"My God!" she whispered.

"You know him?" I asked.

"I don't know him—but I've seen him before," she said.

"Who is he?" Herzog asked.

"I can't tell you that," the girl said. "London, England. Toby was playing a couple of weeks at the Russell Square Hotel. We were living around the corner at a small hotel called Brunswick House. One night—this is about a year ago—Frank and I had stopped somewhere for a late supper. As we walked into Brunswick, there was Toby, masked as always, talking to this man at the bar." She gestured at the body. "Frank didn't seem disturbed as he usually did when strangers glommed onto Toby. I asked Frank who the man was. 'No idea,' Frank told me, 'but Toby gave the all clear on him.' Toby, you understand, Mr. Haskell, never appeared in public with anyone. I suppose there had to be a first time for everything."

"But Frank didn't tell you who he was?"

"He didn't know. Just that Toby had okayed him."

"London police may have his prints and picture," Herzog said. "Thanks, Margaret."

"Everyone calls me Maggie," the girl said.

"Well, Maggie, you've put us on the track, but it may take all day to get any kind of positive results from London."

"I'm not interested in a stranger from London who was dead long before Chambrun was shot," I said. "I'm going to the hospital just in case there are any new reports on Chambrun's condition."

"You may be needed here," Herzog said.

"My personal sanity depends on good news from the hospital," I said.

My personal sanity might depend on good news, but the hospital environment doesn't do much for my general nervous system. I just find myself thanking God that I'm there to visit someone else, not as a patient.

At St. Mark's, I was finally directed to the emergency ward where Chambrun was being held. A nurse sat at a long, narrow, almost tablelike desk. She told me she couldn't give me permission to see Chambrun.

"You'll have to get that from Dr. Lockwood." She nodded toward a white-coated man who was standing at the far end of the desk, studying some medical charts. He looked up at the mention of his name.

"Not much point in going in to see him," he said. "He can't see you."

"You mean . . .?"

"He's, we hope, just temporarily blind," the doctor said.

"Temporarily?"

"I said 'we hope.' He was wearing a hat when he was shot. The inner sweatband—leather—deflected the bullets enough to keep them from going directly into his brain. The nerves controlling his vision are, for now, paralyzed."

"Can he speak—talk?"

"At the moment, he doesn't know if he's alive or dead."

"It might comfort him if he knew I was here to see him," I said. "We're very close."

"A brief visit might help bring him around," Dr. Lockwood said.

He led me down a short corridor and into an unmarked room. Chambrun lay on a bed there, his head swathed in bandages. If he heard us come in, he gave no sign of it. His eyes were closed. I spoke his name. Nothing happened.

"Pierre, it's Mark." I turned to the doctor. "His hearing damaged?"

"We think not," Dr. Lockwood said. "Just overall shock."

I reached down and touched Chambrun's hand. "It's Mark, Pierre." I thought I felt a faint twitching motion in his hand. "I just wanted you to know that we're all pulling for you. We're covering all your duty posts for you."

Again a faint twitch.

"I think he's hearing me," I said to the doctor.

Dr. Lockwood just shrugged.

"Is there anything you can tell us about what happened?" I asked Chambrun. "Did you get a look at the man who shot you?"

No movement. No response of any kind.

"Cops have been burying him under that one," Dr. Lockwood said. "He may not even know what's happened to him."

"You know you were shot, Pierre?" I asked.

No movement or twitch of his hand.

Dr. Lockwood shrugged. "Knowing won't get him better, but you've had more response from him than the lady who was here."

"Miss Ruysdale?"

"I think that was her name. I thought I'd have to bed her down when he didn't respond to her at all."

I turned back to Chambrun. "Did you know Betsy was here, Pierre? She was stunned because you didn't respond to her."

This time his hand seemed almost to writhe under mine.

"I'll tell her you know," I said.

His hand moved again.

"Come back when you can," Dr. Lockwood said. "You may be the medicine he needs. This Ruysdale lady is important to him?"

"Vitally."

"He might show her some signs of life if she'd come back," Dr. Lockwood said. "This can be a minute-to-minute situation."

I hated to leave him, but the answers to too many questions were back at the Beaumont. And Betsy was there. If he was coming around, she was almost certainly the one who could speed it up.

I found Betsy back in her office at the hotel. She was gone almost before I could tell her what his response to hearing her name from me had been. The people I wanted next were Millicent Huber and Colonel Watson. If anyone could fill in Maggie Hanson's story about Toby March giving the dead man in the basement a green light, they were the people to do this.

Watson answered my knock on the door of the room where he and Millicent Huber were registered as Colonel and Mrs. Watson. They were eating breakfast that room service had brought them.

"I've just come from the hospital," I told him, "where

59

Chambrun is showing some very small signs of improvement."

"Glad to hear it," Watson said.

"But I want to talk to you two about something else. You know a girl named Maggie Hanson who's close to Frank Pasqua?"

"I know her well," Millicent said. "She must be out of her mind with anxiety for him."

"She is. But more important, she was able to tell us something about the dead man in the basement."

"She knows him?" Watson asked.

"Not exactly. But she saw him with Toby March in a London hotel. The Brunswick House."

"That's where Toby and Frank and the whole show crew stayed in London."

"And you?" I asked.

"I had my own apartment," she said. "But—I stayed at the Brunswick quite often with Toby."

"Maggie says she saw Toby talking to the man, in the basement, at the Brunswick House bar."

"In public? Never."

"But she says she saw them together. She was with Frank, and he told her that Toby said that the man was free to approach him."

"It just doesn't fit the pattern," Millicent said.

"What pattern?"

"I've already explained to you," Millicent said. "Toby's professional career depends on no one knowing what he really looks like. If you're pretending to be Frank Sinatra or some other famous singer, the listener—the public—has to believe that if that mask came off he would see Frank Sinatra. If he can expect another face, the whole illusion would be spoiled. It's been that way now for years."

"Millicent doesn't even know what Toby looks like," Watson said.

"I first saw him when I was a nurse in the hospital in London. That was when he'd been brought in after his disaster. His face was a mangled mess. We got to be friends—close friends. Then he had plastic surgery done. His face was covered for a month or more after that. It was during that time, his face still covered with bandages, that he told me what he planned to do with his career. Imitations of the famous. He must remain personally anonymous for that to be successful."

"But you," I said. "Why must he remain anonymous to you?"

"It was like some kind of psychosis with him," Watson said. "I met him at the same time, never knew what he looked like before his accident, or after. It's curious how little it matters after a while. When I think of him, I think of bright blue eyes looking out at me through the holes in a black mask. That's what he looks like to me, to Millicent, and to the boys in his band."

"But he is your lover," I said to Millicent.

Her lips twitched. "You don't love a face, you love a person. After a while it didn't matter to me that he had an obsession to keep his looks a secret from the public. His wit, his tenderness, his talent as a lover were all that mattered. If he wanted to keep his looks hidden, it was all right with me. I even understood it after a while."

61

"But to find him, the police need to be able to describe him," I said.

"You think they will find him?" Watson asked.

"That's their business. The hospital in London, the doctor who made over his face, should be able to tell them what they need to know."

"When Frank Pasqua turns up from his 'unfinished business,' he may be able to give them a lead. I think he may be the only person who knows what Toby looks like now. The doctor planned a face for him but how well it turned out, the way he planned it, only he would know if he saw Toby unmasked."

"So give me the hospital's name and the doctor's name," I said. "We'll see what we can dig up on the phone. March hadn't begun to wear a mask while he was still in the hospital, had he?"

"No," Millicent said, "but I think the doctor had agreed to help Toby keep his secret. The secret of his appearance."

"With a possible murder on the books, the doctor wouldn't have to keep that secret," I said.

"You think Toby's been murdered?" Millicent asked.

"The person who lost all that blood in 17C isn't very likely to be alive," I said.

"More likely it is Frank," she said.

"But Frank called Haskell on the phone," Watson said.

"*If* that was Pasqua," I said.

Colonel Watson wrote down the name of the London hospital and the plastic surgeon for me, and I went off to find Lieutenant Herzog. It wasn't much, but it was something.

Herzog and I put through a call to London. The people at

the hospital sure weren't too helpful. They could provide Herzog with fingerprints of the man who had been brought in to them with a ruined face. Dr. Clyde Ferris, the surgeon, gave us very little more. He was a pleasant-sounding Britisher, obviously willing to help but without too much to offer.

"The damage to March's face was almost unbelievable," he said. "I asked him if he had a photograph of himself. He was a public performer. Photographs could be part of his business. But he claimed not to have any. I had to start from scratch."

"March told me that people used to say he looked like Jimmy Stewart," Dr. Ferris continued. "I had to start with something—rebuilding cheekbones, mouth structure, forehead. So I used a photograph of Jimmy Stewart as a guide."

"So he looks like Jimmy Stewart?"

"No way I can tell you," Dr. Ferris said. "He was still a mass of stitches and bandages the last time I saw him. I never saw the final result."

"He left you before the job was completed?"

"Before the results could be seen. Medically, there was no reason he couldn't leave the hospital. I'd have liked to have seen the end results, but it wasn't medically necessary."

"He told you what he planned to do? Keep his identity a secret?"

"And he asked me to play along with him and I agreed. He probably doesn't look any more like Jimmy Stewart than I do. A stranger wouldn't recognize that Jimmy Stewart had been the model for the rebuilding. You understand, I'm only guessing because I don't know what Toby March looks like today."

I sat by the phone in my office, trying to make some sense out of the horrors that had surrounded me since the early-morning hours of Sunday, when Toby March had returned to 17C after his performance in the Blue Lagoon to be confronted by some kind of a deathtrap. Who had been there? We assumed Frank Pasqua. But if the phone call to me, allegedly from Pasqua, had been genuine, then Pasqua hadn't been there. We had assumed that the dead man in the basement had been there, but only because he had been subject to the same kind of wound that had caused someone to bleed so copiously on March's bed. But who and why, no answers.

Then there was Chambrun. Only the miracle of a tough inner hatband had kept two bullets from lodging in his brain. Chambrun hadn't expected anything of that sort. He'd walked out onto the roof unarmed, planning only to scare off an intruder. Neither Betsy Ruysdale nor I knew of any personal feud in his life, any quarrel of deadly proportions, any long-held grudge. Who and why? No answer.

There was no starting point for any of this. I suddenly had a far-out notion. Not even the closest people to Toby March knew what his face looked like. Was it possible the dead man in the basement could be March? Would there be other ways of identifying him besides his face? Surely Millicent Huber, the woman in his life, would have private knowledge of the man if no one else had.

I had some of Jerry's men try to locate Millicent and the four young musicians. They had to have some way of knowing Toby besides his black-masked face.

Millicent, the first to turn up in my office, was outraged at being asked to look at the dead man again and at the suggestion that he might be her man.

"It's absurd, Mr. Haskell," she told me. "Toby's face has never been a part of my life. I would have known, instantly, if the dead man was Toby."

"How?" I asked.

"I—I would have *felt* it. I would have known instantly if the man I love was lying there in front of me, dead."

"You are his lover. You sleep with him," I said. "Are there things aside from his face you would know for certain? A birthmark? The way the hair grows on his chest?"

"I would just know this man isn't Toby!" she said.

"When I was a kid, I had a mole on my chest," I said. "My mother used to call it my 'kissy spot.' If I'd turned up with my face obliterated, she'd have been certain of me by that mole. Is there something unique like that about March?"

"I tell you that man isn't Toby. Nothing will prove he is because I know, deep down, that he isn't."

"And he isn't," a voice said from behind us. It was Ben Lewis, the young guitarist in March's group.

"How do you know that?" I asked him.

"Believe it or not, I had the same notion when you first took me downstairs to look at him," Lewis said, "but almost at once, I knew that was a wild fantasy. The dead man is missing the ring finger of his left hand."

"A recent injury?"

"No. The skin was all grown over, no scars. Probably happened to him when he was a kid. You understand, Mr. Haskell, I've been watching Toby play the piano every day of the week, except Sunday, for the past five years. A jazz pianist has to have a strong left hand. Toby has the greatest I ever saw. No missing finger! His face, which I've never seen, meant nothing to me. But a missing finger he didn't have."

That was the end of that dream. The dead man wasn't Toby March. Millicent Huber left me with a great sigh of relief.

"Any news about Mr. Chambrun?" Ben asked me.

"Pretty bad, but alive and lucky." I told him about the sweatband that had probably saved Chambrun's life.

"You know who had it in for him?" Ben asked.

"No. Not that much 'in for him.' Who had it in for March and Pasqua?" I asked.

Ben's eyes narrowed. "You think they were both attacked, or just one of them?"

"It's hard for me to believe the phone call I got was from Pasqua," I said. "If it was, he wasn't hurt at the time, and he wouldn't have taken what might have happened to March so lightly."

"You asked me before who might have it in for Toby or Frank," Ben said. "Ours is a crazy world. No one feels casual about a star like Toby. They are loved or despised. Not for any sensible reasons, you understand. They are loved because they answered a question in a crowd, or hated because they didn't."

"But in spite of his secret way of living, March must have had close friends," I said. "You spent time with him every day. You must know who those close friends might be."

"Believe it or not, I don't," Ben said. "Pasqua arranges our schedule and where we will stay when we go to some city to play—both here and abroad. If Toby had friends in those places, Pasqua would be instructed to inform them. None of the rest of us knew who they were."

"Staying so anonymous doesn't make sense," I said.

"It's what made his act so perfect," Ben said. "Behind that mask was Frank Sinatra, or Bing Crosby, or Tony Bennett, or whomever he might be impersonating. If it got out that what was really behind that mask was a beat-up Jimmy Stewart, the illusion would be destroyed."

"So one of them was badly hurt. Why would March take Pasqua away, or Pasqua take March away, when help was right at hand? It must be because somewhere there is a friend who would cover for them. But why would Pasqua go that route?" I asked.

"Because he knew that's the way Toby would want it," Ben said.

"Millicent must know," I said.

"If you knew how important it was for Toby to stay anonymous, you would understand how it's possible that the woman who made love with him was just as much in the dark as the rest of us concerning his appearance."

"What about Colonel Watson?" I asked. "You knew him abroad?"

"I never saw him or heard of him until after all this began," Ben told me. "Millicent told me he was a male orderly in the London hospital where Toby went after his face was obliterated. He must be close for Toby to suggest he and Millicent should register as husband and wife."

"That doesn't make any sense to me," I said.

"If it got out that Millicent was Toby's girl, she would have been snowed under by reporters and curious fans. As 'Mrs. Watson,' they'd have no interest in her."

"Could any of the other boys in your orchestra know more than you do?" I asked.

"I'd bet my shirt against it," Ben said.

Dead-end streets no matter where I looked.

Colonel Archibald Watson took me down my last blind alley. He sat opposite me at my desk, with no obvious desire to withhold anything. As I already knew, he'd been a medical orderly at the London hospital where Toby was taken after his disfiguring accident. Watson was called on to help him in and out of wheelchairs when he was well enough, and wheel him around to wherever he wanted to go. Where would he want to go?

"There was a piano in the recreation room," Watson told me. "He wanted to go to it. I knew he was a small-time jazz performer so that didn't surprise me. I wasn't a fan, so I had no way of judging how good he was. But one afternoon, he began to sing along with what he was playing. Something about 'San Francisco.' Suddenly a nurse appeared in the doorway. 'What happened to him?' she asked me. I explained a bus accident and plastic surgery. 'I didn't hear anything about it on the radio or TV,' she said. 'Nothing in the newspapers.' 'Why should there be?' I asked. 'Perry Como.' 'That's not Perry Como,' I told her. 'Of course it is,' she said. 'I'd know his voice anywhere.' "

"I told Toby later," Watson went on. "He was delighted. 'That's who I was when I was singing,' he said. 'She couldn't see any face to contradict what she was hearing. I helped him get his first mask made, one that covered his whole head and the front of his chin and throat. Frank Pasqua, a small-time booking agent who had gotten some of Toby's pre-accident jobs, arranged a tryout of his new act. Toby would be Frank Sinatra for an evening, his face hidden, the sound Sinatra's.

It was a huge success. Millicent and I, who had helped to prepare for it, attended and were impressed. A star was born, and we were a part of it. But friends?" Watson shrugged. "Of course with Millicent it was something else. Their closeness began right there in the hospital. But when I asked her about him, she just shrugged. Toby didn't want to talk about anything but his future. So no past history came up in their conversations. No past loves or close friendships."

"That's hard to accept," I said.

"He'd found a way to build himself a million-dollar future. He didn't want to chance any kind of slip-up."

"What did you and he talk about?" I asked.

"Music—when he talked," Watson said. "I didn't see him very often after he was launched, unless I went to the nightspot where he was working."

"But you came from London to New York to see the opening here. Not very casual, I'd say."

"The booking here at the Beaumont was the top of the ladder to Toby. He wanted us here. And, besides that, I could be helpful. I could register Millicent as my wife, so there would be no way of associating Millicent with him."

"That important?"

"To Toby," Watson said.

"And this last evening?"

"Bing Crosby," Watson said. "You know what a huge send-off he got."

"You didn't see him after the show Saturday night?"

"Only with an army of fans." Watson said. "We made a dinner date because we couldn't talk then."

"So you don't know why it took him so long to go upstairs after he was finished?"

"He could have stayed down until breakfast if he chose to answer all the questions fans wanted to ask him."

"And no clue as to who could have been waiting for him in 17C?"

"Not a clue," Watson said.

The phone on my desk rang. It was Betsy Ruysdale, calling from the hospital.

"It's slow but moving along," she said. "Pierre is able to answer questions by squeezing out a yes or a no with his hand. No speech yet, but the doctor says it's only a matter of hours."

"Great!" I said.

"The trouble is, I'm not asking him the right questions. I thought if you could come over—"

"Of course. I'm taking off right now."

"Pass along my best wishes," Watson said. "Not that he will care. But everyone is the friend of a man who's been attacked by a would-be assassin."

What Betsy had told me on the phone made me feel better, but a look at Chambrun made me feel a hell of a lot better. His facial color was almost back to normal. His dark eyes were bright when he saw me. I sat down beside him and held out my hand. He covered it with an almost firm grip.

"You look as though you are coming along," I told him.

His hand tightened on mine. I told him what I'd been doing—my conversations with Millicent Huber, Ben Lewis, and Watson.

"But they all lead down blind alleys," I told him.

Pierre shook his head from side to side, a feeble motion.

"Are you still thinking that phone call from Pasqua was a fake?" I asked him.

One squeeze of his hand.

"That would mean you think Toby March may be behind some of the violence?"

Again the "yes" squeeze.

"You think March may have taken those shots at you?"

Another single squeeze.

"But you wouldn't have known him if you'd seen him."

Pierre pointed to his stomach.

"But you wouldn't have known him."

He actually jabbed his finger into his stomach.

"You have had a gut feeling about it?"

An almost firm "yes" squeeze.

"But if that's so, Millicent and Colonel Watson could be playing along with him."

A vigorous "yes."

"So I should warn Herzog and Jerry to keep them away from you?"

The single squeeze was almost firm.

"And any strange male should be kept away from you?"

His lips moved. I almost thought he was going to speak, but instead he lay back on his pillow and something very like a smile moved those lips.

"You asked the right questions, got on the right track," Betsy said to me.

Pierre's smile was for real. I couldn't have felt better. We had told ourselves that as a team, Betsy, Jerry, and I would have to try to think his way. I'd made it.

"I'll pass this along to Herzog and Jerry," I told Pierre, giving his hand a last pressure as I stood up.

Betsy followed me out into the hall.

71

"God knows who to be afraid of," she said.

"Any strange male who tries to get to him. The hospital will be wide open to strangers," I said. "We need to get him back to the hotel to keep him completely safe."

"Let me see if I can find Dr. Lockwood for you," Betsy said, and took off.

Even as I waited, two male orderlies went into Pierre's room. I followed them in and waited for whatever they had to do. Medical supplies, clean towels. Pierre could be poisoned if one of those men was a phony—was even March himself, perhaps? That's how helpless we were if he stayed in the hospital.

Dr. Lockwood, a pleasant-looking gray-haired man, heard my story, his good-natured face changing to a dark hardness.

"He shouldn't be moved from here," he said. "It's still pretty touchy. But if the situation is what you say it is—"

"It is. We're all playing blindfolded."

"I can find a young doctor whom I trust and know can't be your Toby March; I can assign him to go back to the hotel with you."

"We'd all breathe easier," I said. "And you might be saving Pierre's life."

"Give me half an hour," Dr. Lockwood said.

He was as good as his word. He turned up with a young doctor named Eric Frost.

"I'll need about an hour to bring Eric up to date on what he needs to know," Lockwood said. "Then we'll send Mr. Chambrun over to the hotel in an ambulance. You'll have that much time to set up shop for him there."

"Thank you, Doctor. I'm sure Pierre would thank you if he could."

"Don't imagine I'd be letting him go if I didn't think it was sound medically, in spite of your ten-twenty-thirty melodrama. Mr. Chambrun may do better for himself in his own bed and with his own people around him."

"You treated his wounds. You know this isn't any fake melodrama," I said.

"Of course I know," Dr. Lockwood said. He and Frost went into Chambrun's room, and I headed back for the Beaumont.

"If the boss is well enough to come back here, we should begin to feel better," Jerry Dodd said when I'd brought him and Lieutenant Herzog up to date.

"I'm not sure Chambrun will be safer here," Herzog said. "This is the crossroads of the world at the moment."

"I'll put every man I have around his penthouse if it is necessary," Jerry said.

"You really think the Huber woman and Colonel Watson are in the act?" Herzog asked me.

"Chambrun does and so do I," I said. "Won't the London police tell you what they can find out about them—if they have records?"

"I'll get on that at once," Herzog said. "How do you keep them away from Chambrun without letting them know what you suspect?"

"Medical explanations," I said.

"I'll have them covered," Herzog said. "If they know where March is, they may lead us to him sooner or later."

"I hope you're not dreaming," Jerry said.

"That means we must keep them from guessing that we're on to them," Herzog said.

That was put to the test almost at once. As I was leaving my office to head for the roof and the penthouse, I came face to face with the colonel and Millicent in the lobby. I'd had no particular emotion about those two before now. Now I felt a deep rage at the sight of them. If Chambrun was right, they were in cahoots with Toby March.

"What's the news at the hospital?" Watson asked me in a relaxed tone.

"Not speaking. Not communicating in any fashion," I said, lying my head off. I could almost feel the squeeze of Chambrun's hand.

"If there was anything we could do to make things easier for him," Millicent said.

"I don't think he'd know you if he saw you," I said.

"But he knew you?" Watson asked.

"I think so. And Betsy. But we are the closest people in the world to him," I said.

"Nothing about the man who shot him?" Watson asked.

"Wouldn't have been even if the guy had missed," I said. "It was still dark when the shots were fired. The shape of a man, perhaps, but nothing by which to identify him."

"Bad break," Watson said.

I didn't mention Chambrun's finger pointing at his stomach—his "gut feeling."

"Let us know if there is anything new," Millicent said. "If there is nursing help needed, that has been my life, you know."

2

London turned lives upside down a few hours later. Lieutenant Herzog came charging into my office in the late afternoon.

"We got lucky," he told me. "I sent the fingerprints of the dead man in the basement to Scotland Yard. The dead man is a London cop—Inspector Jason Claridge."

"So what was he doing here?"

"Terrorists," Herzog said.

"Meaning?"

"Half a dozen Britishers in high places were taken hostage a few months ago. The price of a release for them was the turning free of some characters the British are holding. As I understand it, it has something to do with Iran and the war there. Inspector Claridge's job was to find the kidnapped Britishers and free them. The trail brought him here to New York."

"So he had information that could lead you to his killers?" I asked.

"If he had, he hadn't passed it back to his headquarters."

"So all you have is a reason for his being here?"

"All I have on the dead man," Herzog said. "Your friends — Colonel Watson and Miss Huber — are real enough. They both worked at the London hospital at the time Toby March was brought there with a smashed face. They both quit their jobs shortly after March was released. London thinks they cared for March while he was there and were persuaded to take on the job of caring for him privately when he left."

"What has that got to do with hostages?" I asked.

"Maybe nothing, maybe everything. Enough to cost Inspector Claridge his life!"

"So what's next?"

"I've ordered my men to get Watson and Miss Huber up here so we can talk with them."

"They should be bringing Chambrun here any time now," I said.

"He can hear what they have to say, even if he can't question them," Herzog said. "Watson and the woman smell too fishy not to be involved in Chambrun's theory about Toby March."

"Doesn't it occur to you, Lieutenant, that the reason Chambrun was shot was because he was pushing the idea that Toby March is the villain of the piece?"

"It has occurred to me," Herzog said. "It also occurs to me that Watson and Miss Huber can tell us exactly where March and Frank Pasqua are hiding."

Five minutes later, two uniformed cops brought Watson and Miss Huber into Chambrun's penthouse.

"I'd like to know just what the hell this is all about," Watson said. "I was told if we didn't come up here voluntarily, Miss Huber and I would be placed under arrest."

"Did you think of not coming?" Herzog asked him.

"Of course I thought of it," Watson said. "I don't like being shuffled around like a piece in a puzzle by cops who don't know which end is up."

"Oh, come off it, Colonel. Miss Huber is Toby March's girl. You are his friend and her friend. March has disappeared, leaving behind him a scene of violence. The dead man we found in the basement turns out to be a London cop, Inspector Jason Claridge. Name mean anything to you?"

"Never heard of him," Watson said.

"You, Miss Huber?"

"I have never heard of him," Millicent Huber said, "and I never saw him before the view we had of him in the basement."

"What is this English cop doing here?" Watson asked.

"Looking for someone involved in the kidnapping and holding as hostages of some British bigshots," Herzog said.

"Let the British cops handle it," Watson said. "As you Americans would say, it's their ball game."

At that moment, the door to the penthouse opened and two uniformed policemen walked in at the front end of a stretcher on which Chambrun lay, flat on his back. Another two uniformed men brought up the rear.

"We can't have any strangers in here without searching them for weapons," Herzog said. He ordered one of the cops to search the colonel.

Watson backed away. "Now wait a minute!" he said. "You can't search me without a warrant."

"If it's necessary, handcuff him," Herzog ordered his man. The colonel shrugged and stood still. The cop felt him, front and back.

"All clear, Lieutenant," the cop said.

"Fine. Now the lady. Hand over your purse, please, Miss Huber."

"Then one of your men gets a free feel. Is that it?" Watson asked.

"Dirty-minded son of a bitch," a clear voice said behind me.

I turned. Chambrun was leaning up on one elbow, looking as surprised as I was. He let himself down to lay flat again, his eyes closed.

"I owe you a debt of thanks, Colonel," he said, in a perfectly normal voice. "Your surliness seems to have restored my power to speak."

There was something a little pornographic about watching the cop go over Millicent Huber's very feminine curves feeling for a gun.

"Don't you search Haskell?" Watson asked.

"I'm not a stranger," I said. "You want to take Mr. Chambrun to his bedroom? It's just down the hall here. Follow me."

Betsy Ruysdale was already in the bedroom turning down the bedclothes. The uniformed cops lifted Chambrun off the stretcher and put him gently down on the bed. Chambrun glanced up at Betsy and me. "I don't understand what unbuttoned me," he said. "I feel as though someone had drilled a well in my head."

"You'd never have let the colonel get away with that kind of ugly implication under normal conditions," I said. "I like to think that was a sign that things are getting back to normal."

"I hear you are talking," a voice at the door said. It was Dr. Lockwood from the hospital. "Something scare you, Mr. Chambrun?"

"Something made me angry," Chambrun said.

"We never know what will start things moving," the doctor said. "We are grateful for anything that does."

"Can I talk with Lieutenant Herzog?" Chambrun asked.

"Why not? It might speed you along. If you have the impulse to get up and walk to the john, or look at the view from your windows, it's okay. I'm leaving a nurse, Miss Caldwell, here to pick you up if you fall."

Victoria Haven came in from the front rooms. "Thank God you are coming around, Pierre," she said. "When I saw that man trying to look in your windows, I should have called security, not you. I should have known you wouldn't take a threat to yourself seriously enough. I'd never forgive myself if it had turned out worse."

"We couldn't have waited for someone to come up from the lobby level, love," Chambrun said.

"Not if you wanted to risk getting yourself killed."

"We should cherish that hat I was wearing," Chambrun said. He turned his head to look at Herzog, who had joined us. "I could hear before the colonel released my speech ducts, Lieutenant. The dead man was a British cop?"

"Inspector Claridge, Scotland Yard," Herzog said. "It seems the British arrested about a dozen Iranians who were guilty of bombing some allied ships in the Persian Gulf. The Iranians retaliated by snatching six high-up Britishers — not in the Gulf, but on English territory. They are the price for the Iranian prisoners. The British don't want it that way, but they want their own people back. That was Claridge's job."

79

"But what was Claridge doing here in New York?"

"He evidently thought the Britishers had been brought here, or he had a lead to someone he thought was responsible for snatching them."

"Who did he talk to here?"

"We're trying to track that information down," Herzog said.

"Not you, Mark?" Chambrun asked me.

"I never saw him until I saw him dead in the basement," I replied.

"Why would you think he might have been talking to Haskell?" Herzog asked.

"If he was trying to locate someone he thought might be staying at the Beaumont, Mark would be the one to ask," Chambrun said.

"We've had a solid English group here, or people who have lived important parts of their lives in England," Herzog said. "Toby March, Frank Pasqua, Colonel Watson, and Miss Huber."

"You think Claridge was killed in March's suite?" Chambrun said. "We can't ask either March or Pasqua about him until you find them. Watson and Miss Huber have already denied ever having seen the inspector before, which certainly means they didn't talk to him."

"If you can believe them," Herzog said.

"Can you?"

"I don't believe anyone who can be a suspect in a murder," Herzog said.

The phone rang on Chambrun's bedside table. Betsy answered it.

"It's for you, Lieutenant," she said to Herzog. "London calling you."

Herzog took the phone and listened to a long conversation from overseas.

"Thanks for calling," he said finally. "At this point, the man is missing." He put the phone down. "Scotland Yard," he said. "A friend of Claridge's reports that he was looking for Toby March overseas. That he came to New York because he heard March was opening here at the Beaumont."

"On the basis of that, we could make a guess," Chambrun said.

"So guess," Herzog said.

"Claridge came here looking for Toby March," Chambrun said. "Why, we don't know. When he got here, March had already started his evening performance in the Blue Lagoon. Claridge found out where March was bedded down, came up to 17C and let himself in. No problem for an experienced cop, picking a lock. Along around two-thirty, Pasqua came up to his room, which adjoins 17C and had been set up so he could walk into 17C from his room. He goes in and finds Claridge there. Pasqua knew who Claridge was, or found out from talking with him. Maybe Pasqua tried to get away and Claridge tried to stop him, an act in which Pasqua was badly hurt and left to bleed to death on March's bed. March walks in on that bloody violence, and he and Claridge have a go at it."

"Does no one have a gun?" Herzog asked.

"Not handy, apparently. My recollection is that British cops don't walk around armed."

"So keep guessing," Herzog said.

"Whether March had a gun or just used a fireplace tool, he managed to put Claridge out of business permanently. What next? March must get rid of Claridge's body so it won't be found in 17C. The security men are no longer in the hallway outside. The press and March's fans are long gone. The elevators are self-service after midnight. March drags the body out to an elevator and takes it down to the basement. Then he goes back to 17C to help his friend. Whether Pasqua can help at all to get away, we still have to guess."

"Why take him away?" Herzog asked. "Why not get help here in the hotel?"

"If Pasqua was hurt so badly that he was babbling about facts that mustn't be spilled to strangers, March would have to get him away or keep him silent."

"Talk about the British hostages?"

"What else? Claridge didn't travel thousands of miles to gossip with March. He must have had reason to believe that March could lead him to the men he wanted to free."

"So that's where they are? Where the hostages are being held?"

"As good a guess as any, wouldn't you say?" Chambrun asked.

"So how do we go about finding that place?" Herzog asked.

"There is one person, maybe two, who could tell us," Chambrun said. "Millicent Huber would know. In all likelihood, Colonel Watson knows, too."

"How do we get them to talk?" Herzog asked.

Chambrun hesitated and then looked at me. "Mark is a wonderful soft talker. It's just possible he could trip her into making a mistake."

"Not likely," I said. "There could be hundreds of thousands of dollars involved. People don't get careless under those conditions."

"You think that kind of money is involved?" Herzog asked.

"A seven-year war is on the line," Chambrun said. "Iran would pay a fortune to keep those Britishers available for a deal that will get their own people back."

"Talk to the lady as casually as you can, Mark," Chambrun said. "Maybe something will slip."

The identity of the dead man in the basement was no longer a secret from the American press or the curious public. The first news that the Britishers being held hostage included royalty—a prince, a duke, and an earl—turned out not to be true. There were, it seems, eleven hostages, all teenage children of British political figures. There had been seven boys and four girls. One of the girls had been returned, dead, to her family's home more than a month ago. She had been raped and brutally beaten. With her was a message that warned that the other young people would receive similar treatment if Iranian prisoners weren't returned to their homeland. It has been the policy of Western allies, right down the line, not to be stampeded into releasing legitimately taken prisoners of war under threat. Finding out where the remaining ten young people were being held, and by whom, had been Inspector Claridge's assignment. He must have come close, we thought, or why else all the commotion and his murder?

One thing seemed to be certain to us. There was no place you could hide ten teenagers, as a group, in the Beaumont. Each one of them must be being held separately if they were anywhere in our hotel, and by now the search had been so thorough we had to believe for certain that they were not with us.

My assignment—to find and talk with Millicent Huber—turned out not to be too difficult. The lady was in the lobby level Spartan Bar having a drink with Colonel Watson. They offered no objection to my joining them at their table.

"This news must be distressing Mr. Chambrun," Watson said. "His theory that Toby is criminally involved must be blown sky-high by now."

"How so?" I asked him.

"Nothing in the world would persuade Toby to launch some kind of attack against British people," Watson said. "He feels an enormous debt to them. They took care of him while he was hurt. British medicine restored his face. British musicians and British show-business people got him launched in his new act, which has been a sensation. Toby owes, and owes, and owes them."

"Nothing? I've heard talk of hundreds of thousands of dollars," I said. "That wouldn't tempt him?"

"You don't know him or you wouldn't ask that," Millicent Huber said. "Toby's sense of loyalty to friends is one of the certain things about him."

"You know how much you're paying him here at the Beaumont?" Watson asked.

I nodded. "Ten thousand a week—for two weeks," I said.

"That's half a million for a year, which is probably what he makes. I don't think he could be tempted to risk his life and future for a criminal act for strangers he doesn't know. He has no connection with Iran. I could swear he has no Iranian friends."

"And for certain he wouldn't rape an English girl," Millicent said.

"Inspector Claridge must not have seen it that way," I said. "Or why would he have come here looking for March?"

"Do you know that he came here looking for Toby?" Watson asked. "Or is that just one of Chambrun's guesses?"

"Well—"

"He came here looking for hostages," Watson said. "Only Chambrun, and some suckers like you whom he's convinced, will ever buy Chambrun's story. Toby's debt to the British is far too great for him ever to wage any kind of war against them."

"Where would this man of many friends and many loyalties take a wounded Frank Pasqua to hide him?" I asked. "Some doctor friend? Some friend with luxurious accommodations who owes him?"

Watson looked up at the ceiling. "You've swallowed Chambrun's theory that the call you got Sunday from Frankie was a fake?" he asked.

"Not at the time I got the call. Later—well—"

"When you got the call you believed what you were told. It was Frank Pasqua. He'd seen something about some trouble at the Beaumont on TV, or maybe on the radio, and he was sure Toby March could take care of himself. You thought the 'unfinished business' he mentioned was some girl."

"True."

"If it was a girl, and his business with her was unfinished, he wouldn't have been listening to the radio or TV all this time. That would explain why he hasn't checked back in.

85

Monday is the day he is supposed to check in for work. When he does, that's when he'll find out what has been going on and he'll kick himself for not having checked back in earlier."

"If he isn't the guy who must have come close to bleeding to death in 17C," I said.

"Oh, brother!" Watson said.

"You don't see Maggie Hanson hanging around here anywhere, do you?" Millicent asked.

It had been my assignment to get Millicent to talk. So far she hadn't, but she appeared to have agreed with everything Watson had had to say.

"If she was concerned about Frank, she'd be somewhere around the Beaumont, wouldn't she?" Millicent asked.

"Maybe she doesn't want to find out what the unfinished business is," I said.

"Some other dame?" Watson suggested.

"Or dying," I said. "Everybody's unfinished business."

"But Frank wouldn't give that meaning to it in a cheerful telephone call!" Watson said.

"Maybe not," I said. "But tell me. You're probably as prone to guessing as anyone. Give me your guess as to why Inspector Claridge came here to the Beaumont."

"It's no guess," Watson said. "He was looking for the British hostages and their captors."

"And he suspected Toby and Frank. That's why he went up to 17C?"

" 'Suspect' is the wrong word," Watson said. "He hoped he could get help from them in finding the British hostages."

"Help?"

"There was some kind of equivalent of one of your country fairs down in Farmington, England," Watson said. "One of the entertainers was Toby March. Those eleven British youngsters were there as a group, representing some kind of young people's club. They never got home from the fair. Claridge hoped Toby or Frank might have noticed someone paying particular attention to the kids, talking to them, trying to be friendly."

"And that is your guess?"

"It's not a guess," Watson said. "Claridge told me, asked me the same question. Millicent and I were there at that fair, watching Toby perform."

"But you said you didn't know Claridge, had never seen him before when they took you to the basement to look at his body!"

"At that time, I thought the whole business of the hostages might be an important secret—important to their safety. Scotland Yard could make it public if they chose to."

"What else have you not told us that we need to know?" I asked. I was more than slightly burned.

"There were ten young lives at stake," Watson said. "I've straightened it out with Lieutenant Herzog."

"He knows that you lied when you and Millicent said you'd never seen Claridge before?" Mark asked.

"I didn't lie," Millicent said. "I hadn't ever seen him before. Archie didn't tell me what he knew until after we'd first been asked to look at the body—after he'd told Herzog why he hadn't publicly identified the inspector."

"So, are you willing to say now where Toby is and where he may be hiding a wounded Frank Pasqua?" I asked.

"No idea," Watson said.

"And I'm supposed to believe that, or are you saving someone in danger?"

"I'm telling you we don't know—where they are or if Frank is hurt," Watson said, his parting words as he and Millicent left the Spartan Bar.

Lieutenant Herzog confirmed part of Watson's story. After he, Herzog, had let it be known what he'd heard from England about who Claridge was and why he might be here, Watson had come to him to say his denial that he knew who Inspector Claridge was a falsehood, and why he'd gone that route.

"Pretty thin, I must say," Herzog said. "But making it public could conceivably have endangered those hostage kids. It could have put Watson himself in danger, but he never suggested that."

"So you don't think he's holding out on where March and Pasqua are holed up? They're close friends, Watson and the missing pair."

"We're having them watched," Herzog said. "Watson's too smart not to guess that, and that we'll be trying to cover any phone calls. But we'll keep at it."

"There is no point in my trying to get Millicent to talk," I said. "Whatever she says will be what they want me to believe, not the truth."

"God help us, I think it's likely that somewhere in the hotel there is a clue to those British hostages," Herzog said.

"And that Chambrun was close, or else why shoot him?" I said.

We just stared at each other. Answers were so close—and yet not ripe for the picking.

I'm happy to report that as the day moved on, Chambrun seemed to be improving rapidly. He was out of bed and sitting up in a reclining chair by midafternoon. Toward the end of the day, he was walking to the bathroom, unaccompanied. He ate a buffet supper with what looked like a normal appetite.

"Back to the regular grind tomorrow, Mark," he said, just before he headed back to bed for the night.

We weren't letting him sleep unwatched. Two cops were stationed in the living room. The recliner was moved into the little dressing room, and I took over there. I could almost hear Chambrun's breathing. Two more cops were stationed in the kitchen area. No one was going to get to our man. I don't think I slept at all, just dozed. I know I wasn't shocked when Herzog burst into my little cubicle. The gray light of dawn was at the windows.

"We've been hit again," Herzog said.

"Hit?"

"Like the music, murder goes round and round," Herzog said. "A young boy who was one of the hostages."

"How do you know that?" I asked.

"About an hour ago, we got a group picture from Scotland Yard of the kids who were abducted," Herzog said. "This one's name is Douglas White, and he's the son of Britain's ambassador to one of the Middle East countries. Stabbed to death in the pantry off our lobby grillroom, with a carving knife from our supplies. Several times in the stomach and chest, and his throat was cut.

"Sons of bitches," Chambrun said from the doorway. He'd evidently heard everything Herzog had to say. His face was ash white.

"There is a note for you, Mr. Chambrun," the detective said. He fished a piece of plain white paper out of his pocket and then read it aloud.

Mr. Chambrun:

Get out of the act unless you want your hotel turned into a cemetery for the other nine hostages. We warned the English swine that if they didn't turn our people loose by dawn, we'd present them with another body. We don't make idle threats.

"It's not signed," Herzog said.

"You say this boy was found in the grillroom pantry? How did the body get there with the place under your surveillance?" Chambrun asked.

"Guessing games again," Herzog said. "We think the White boy was brought there to the grillroom pantry and killed there. Just walked in from outside somewhere, to the basement, and brought up to the lobby level in an elevator."

"Without crying out for help or trying to get away?"

"He could have been warned that if he tried to attract attention to himself, he'd pay for it. So White let himself be walked away from wherever he was being held and eventually wiped out."

"Whoever handled this, if that's the way it was," Chambrun said, "has to know the hotel pretty well—where elevators will take them, where they'll find a usable weapon."

"You wouldn't have to have a map drawn," Herzog said. "Just walk around a little."

"Right under our noses," Chambrun said. "I wish to God that I was in the act deep enough to be a threat to them. Enough has come out now that my guesses aren't very dangerous."

"We can redouble our surveillance," Herzog said. "But I don't think they're likely to walk into a trap."

"You say Scotland Yard sent you a photograph of the missing kids?"

"They were photographed as a group sometime before they went to that fair where March was entertaining. It's downstairs in your office. Not that it will do you any good, except to wring your heart. So young, so very alive! The only thing of interest is that that fair was held in the same town where March went to a convalescent home after his face was fixed."

"Watson and Miss Huber again," Chambrun said. "They worked there. They must have seen someone."

"The dead boy's father, Anthony White, is on his way here from London," Herzog said. "He should arrive here in about an hour. I don't envy him having to look at what's left of his boy."

"Murdering butchers," Chambrun said. "I'd like to see for myself."

"Can you make it?" Herzog asked.

"I can do anything or go anywhere that will get us closer to the people we want," Chambrun said.

In his office downstairs was the picture of the young people who'd been taken hostage.

"The one to the right of center is Douglas White," Herzog said, handing the picture to Chambrun. I looked over his shoulder at it. They were all so young. The White boy was blond, with a nice friendly smile.

"Let's get Watson and Miss Huber here," Chambrun said.

The two were in the room where they were registered as husband and wife. Millicent Huber seemed shaken. "Three of those kids had seen Toby," she said. "Someone had recommended him as a possible entertainer for their fair."

"Then they would know March by sight," Herzog said.

Millicent shook her head. "He was into his mask routine," she said. "He sang for them—his Bing Crosby, his Sammy Davis, Jr., his Frank Sinatra. They were enchanted and hired him to work at the fair two days later. He had already put together the four boys who were to act as his musical backup."

"Did March know who these kids were who wanted to hire him, who their important families were?" Chambrun asked.

"They told him," Millicent said. "They couldn't afford the fee he was asking from them, but they suggested that if he was a success their families might offer him a dozen jobs later on.

"In the end, the White boy's father, Anthony White auditioned Toby. When he heard Toby play and sing, he offered to put up the money for the original fee he had asked for."

"So Anthony White saw him?"

"Not without the mask," Millicent said. "He wasn't appearing anywhere without the mask by that time."

"But by now he knew how important these kids and their parents were," Chambrun said.

"You still playing that tune?" Watson asked. "You're suggesting he planned the kidnapping right then?"

"He didn't need a special place to plan it," Chambrun said. "He only had to be able to convince the buyer that he could produce something to sell!"

"Nonsense," Watson said.

"Mr. White may be able to help us when he gets here," Chambrun said. "He may be able to help us identify March by clothing, some mannerism he noticed. That I'm sure you won't do, Colonel. You and Miss Huber are March's close friends."

I had no idea at all what kind of special thing might help identify a maskless March. One thing seemed certain, the Colonel and Millicent Huber could identify him, mask or no mask. Whether they knew where he was operating from now, holding the hostages, hiding Frank Pasqua was something else. As you can see, I was beginning to buy Chambrun's theory in larger chunks. It was possible, I told myself, that March's two friends didn't know where his headquarters were. It would be dangerous for them to know. They might unintentionally give him away.

Anthony White arrived at the Beaumont a little after noon on Tuesday. He was taken at once to identify his son. The experience was obviously almost too much for him. He was fence-paint white when Herzog brought him to Chambrun's office, and shaking from head to foot. He couldn't control his cultivated British voice. We were like a little corner of London there in the office. Mr. White, Colonel Watson, and Millicent all had British accents, and Chambrun's cultivated way of talking wasn't far off. The colonel and Millicent were on hand because they'd been present when Mr. White had made the deal for Toby March's services.

"The only thing bearable about the situation is that it must have been quick," Anthony White said to Chambrun after they had been introduced.

"No doubt he's your son, Mr. White?"

"Oh, my God!"

"There are seven stomach and chest wounds," Herzog said. "Any one of them could have been fatal, according to Dr. Partridge." He glanced at Mr. White. "The throat slashing was just window-dressing. The boy was long gone before that took place."

"If I ever get my hands on that killer, I'll kill him with my bare hands," Mr. White said. "You really believe it may be Toby March, Mr. Chambrun?"

"Guesswork, but I believe it," Chambrun said. "If not, where is he, and why hasn't he asked for help?"

"Bastard!" Mr. White said. "What would his connection be with Iran? He's an American, isn't he? I talked to him in England, you know. Made a deal with him for Douglas and his group. I thought he was just an entertainer."

"And that's all he is," Watson said. "Mr. Chambrun is way out in left field on this. Toby is a decent, law-abiding man, who would never make a deal to work for terrorists."

"I know that's true, Mr. White," Millicent said.

"You were a nurse there at the hospital, weren't you, Miss Huber?" Mr. White asked.

"Yes. I took care of Toby from the day he was brought in with his face destroyed. We got to be very close. I got to know him too well to believe for an instant that Toby would have sold out those British kids for money or ever, ever be involved with a brutal butchering."

"But the White boy was butchered and March has evaporated," Chambrun said. "Frank Pasqua is missing, too. He didn't turn up for breakfast Monday as he assured us he would."

"You think they are in this together?" White asked. "As I recall, Pasqua handled all of March's business affairs. I know he dealt with me about the performance at the fair in Farmington where they all met."

"They could be a team," Chambrun said. "Or Pasqua may be another victim."

"March would turn on his own friends?"

"When a man turns into a bloody psycho," Chambrun said, "there is no rational explanation for any of his behavior."

"Toby was the victim of a criminal act by the person who threw a bomb into the bus and caused his terrible injuries."

"And what has happened to Frank Pasqua is an accident, not a crime?" Chambrun asked.

"Of course. Frank found himself a dame that is absorbing his attention," Watson said.

" 'Unfinished business.' He's got unfinished business here if Toby doesn't show up for tonight's performance in the Blue Lagoon."

"Toby is a grown man," Watson said. "He'll show up where he's supposed to be."

"Want to bet on it?" Chambrun asked.

"Of course I'll bet on it. Fifty bucks suit you?"

"Just fine," Chambrun said.

"What do you think has happened to him?" Mr. White asked.

"March? I think he is carrying out a campaign of abduction and terror for which he is being well paid by Iranian monsters," Chambrun answered.

"You just assume that," Millicent Huber said, her voice rising to something like anger for the first time. "You don't know a thing about Toby as a human being."

"Tell me," Chambrun said.

"I'd never seen him or met him until he became my patient," Millicent said. "But as you are aware, I got to know him very well. He was a badly injured man who took his tragic accident with great courage. I would use the word 'gallantry' if I knew exactly how to define it. It was 'just one of those things,' Toby said. He was a gentle and tender man."

"You made that easy, I suspect," Chambrun said.

"I—I was attracted to him," Millicent said. "Yes, I played along with the man-woman relationship he wanted and needed. I've never regretted it. I never saw anything that suggested he was capable of violence or ugly rage. He could no more kill Douglas White the way you've described it than fly to the moon. It's laughable to think of him being paid for violence."

"And you wound up in his bed?"

"The happiest days of my life," Millicent said.

"And you, Watson, what did you see in the man?" Chambrun asked.

"He handled what happened to him with more guts than I could have churned up if it had happened to me. If you could have seen his face and known the pain he suffered.

The loss to his pride, too. He told me he was a good-looking guy before the accident. Now he had to look in the mirror at raw meat."

"And wanted to get back at the world," Anthony White said. "I think I understand how he must have felt." His fists were tightly clenched. "If I ever get the chance—"

"Toby never spoke one word to me about getting even," Watson said.

"This other man, his partner?" Mr. White asked. "His name is Pasqua?"

"Maggie Hanson, Pasqua's girl, is down in the lobby waiting for him to get back from his 'unfinished business,'" Herzog said. "Shall I get her up here?"

Chambrun nodded. Somehow I didn't think he'd been sold on the "good guy" account of Toby March. Neither had Anthony White.

"These people were March's friends," Mr. White said. "The lady was his love life. But Scotland Yard took other aspects of him seriously enough to send Inspector Claridge across the Atlantic to have a look at him."

"And possibly his partner," Herzog said.

Jerry Dodd had left us to go find Maggie Hanson in the lobby. Mr. White was right, of course. You couldn't expect anything but a biased report about March from his woman and one of his few friends.

Maggie evidently hadn't been hard to find because Jerry returned with her in what seemed only a minute or two later. She wasn't the only person he brought. Young Ben Lewis, the guitarist in March's musical group, was also with him.

"I thought Lewis might give us something on both men," he said to Herzog.

Young Lewis seemed to be focused on Anthony White. "They just told me about your son, sir. God, how terrible for you. I got to know him back in England when we signed up to play for the fair in Farmington. I don't know anything to say to you, sir."

"Thanks for wanting to try," Mr. White said.

"I remember how enthusiastic your son was about Toby's act, particularly the Sammy Davis, Jr., segment of it."

"He—he loved music," Mr. White said. "Made a fan of me. I remember being outraged by the fee March was asking— five hundred pounds for three performances at a charity function. But when I heard you all play and heard him sing, I put up the lacking funds out of my own pocket."

"How good he was as a performer isn't a matter for debate," Colonel Watson said.

"I should think not, at his prices," Mr. White said.

"They are considerably more today than you paid in England," I told him.

"So money isn't a problem with him," Mr. White said.

"That depends on what money means to you," Chambrun said. "A thousand dollars for a performance is one thing. A half million for an act of violence is another. You haven't heard from Pasqua, Miss Hanson?"

"Nothing from him or about him since the call Mr. Haskell had from him," Maggie replied.

"*If* that was from him," Chambrun said. "We've been playing with the idea that it could have been March imitating your man. How did they get on together—your man and Toby March?"

"It was totally a business relationship at first," Maggie said.

"Frank was working for a talent agent in London when Toby found him. Frank quit his job and took over the management of Toby's act. They became close friends."

"And nobody else?" Chambrun asked.

"Nobody else," the girl said.

"Do you know what his salary is?"

"He works on a percentage basis," Maggie said. "You know what he's getting here at your hotel. Frank gets ten percent of it."

"Two hundred dollars a night," Chambrun said. He was passing on information to the others. Of course I knew.

"Aren't you distressed that you haven't heard from him?" Mr. White asked.

"I'm angry. But distressed, of course, after what I've heard."

"If he had some kind of 'unfinished business,' when should he turn up to handle the business he has here?"

"An hour before show time," Maggie said. "That would be at eight o'clock. He would check on Ben and the other musicians, make sure the set was properly arranged, piano in the right place, proper programs ready to distribute — those sorts of things."

"And Toby should show up — when?" Chambrun asked.

"Ten minutes to nine, just before show time."

"Is that time enough for him to get into costume?"

"He dresses in his room, wherever he is staying. Comes to the theater masked and ready."

"So we just wait for things to turn normal?" Mr. White asked.

"That's something we wait for, which I doubt very much will happen," Chambrun said.

"Still guessing?" Mr. White asked.

"Putting two and two together and trying to come up with something other than four," Chambrun said. "You ever know Inspector Claridge, Maggie?"

"The man they found dead in the basement?"

"Did you and Frank know him in London or anywhere in England?"

Maggie's shoulders shivered. "I saw him talking to Toby at the bar in the Russell Square Hotel in London," she said.

"Frank?"

"Well, of course, we haven't had a chance to talk about it. But he's never mentioned a Scotland Yard inspector to me."

"He wouldn't mention a cop he saw on the street corner every day unless there was something special about him," Chambrun said.

"What do you think the 'four' will look like?" Mr. White asked.

Chambrun hesitated and then spoke in a calm, very level voice. "After the performance Saturday night, Frank Pasqua went up to his room, which adjoins 17C. It is set up so that he could walk from his own room into Toby's suite. That was about two-thirty. Jerry Dodd's man saw him. I'm guessing that he went into March's room for something perfectly ordinary and found Inspector Claridge waiting there. Maybe he knew him, maybe he got to know him. Got to know him and why he was there. Toby was suspected of being involved in the abduction of Douglas White and his friends."

"Frank wouldn't have believed that for an instant," Colonel Watson said.

"Unless Claridge had some proof for him."

"Frank wouldn't even have believed proof," Watson said.

"Let's say it went this way," Chambrun said. "Claridge told Frank his story, and they waited for March to make an appearance. When he did, Pasqua told him what Claridge had claimed to be the facts. March wandered around until he got to the fireplace, snatched up the iron poker, and attacked Claridge with it. Pasqua tried to stop him and got clipped with the poker. Then Claridge got the blows that killed him. March was confronted with a dead man and one unconscious and bleeding seriously. He puts the bleeding Pasqua on the bed and tries to figure out what to do. He has time, hours before the maid will come in the morning to make up the room. He takes Claridge's body out, to the elevators. Jerry Dodd's man had already gone. There wouldn't be any more curious fans snooping around at that time of the morning. He takes the body down to the basement and leaves it, where it was later found. Pasqua was more of a problem. He could leave him where he was to bleed to death, but Pasqua was his friend. Maybe he could be persuaded to keep his mouth shut, perhaps share in the proceeds from Iran. But he had to get Pasqua somewhere he could talk to him in private, where he wouldn't spill the beans to Herzog or his cops. Where, is the question. Because that's where he and Pasqua are now. Could Pasqua be bought? If he could, he may be alive. If he couldn't, God help him."

"And the phone call to Haskell?" Watson asked.

"To keep us from looking for Pasqua, or connecting his absence with the violence in 17C," Chambrun said. "What do you think, Miss Hanson? Would Frank go along with March for a six-figure bribe—say, a hundred grand?"

"I don't think so," the girl said. "He detested violence and would never let himself become a party to it."

"Then I'm afraid we have to assume that Pasqua is dead," Chambrun said. "Our second murder."

"Your next whodunit should make the bestseller list," Watson said in an angry voice. "You choose to accept Maggie's assessment of Frank's character, and refuse to accept Millicent's and mine about Toby."

"Tell the story some other way," Chambrun suggested.

Watson drew a deep breath. "I go along with you on how they came together," he said. "Frank finds Claridge in 17C and hears his story. The fact is that it is Frank who's been dealing with the Iranians. While they are having it out, Toby arrives and hears what's up. It is Frank who picks up the fireplace poker and attacks Claridge. It is Toby who is wounded and left bleeding. Claridge is killed. But the killer is Frank Pasqua. He can't let the inspector be found or Toby either. He takes Claridge's body down to the basement. Then he takes Toby someplace where he can be hidden and cared for, hoping he can bribe Toby to keep his mouth shut. So Toby March wouldn't buy, and he is now dead, our second murder, and Frank is the killer."

"No! Never!" Maggie Hanson cried out.

"It goes just as well that way as the other," Watson said.

"Except for one thing," Chambrun said. "Scotland Yard didn't mention Pasqua to Lieutenant Herzog. Only March."

"Toby and Pasqua operated like one to people who didn't know them," Watson said. "If someone from Iran visited the place in London where Toby and Frank lived, they would assume Frank was there to visit Toby. Frank, to them, would have appeared to be just a working stiff."

"It could also be true about the moon and green cheese," Chambrun said.

"Did you ever see anyone who could have been Iranian hanging around the place where March and Pasqua lived in London?" Herzog asked Ben Lewis.

"We never hung around that place ourselves," Ben said. "We met Toby at the place where we were going to perform that night, planned the program, rehearsed there. We had no reason to go to the place where he lived. We had no problems that needed private discussion."

"And the phone call to Haskell about 'unfinished business.' Could March have imitated Pasqua?" Herzog asked.

"He could have imitated God if he knew what he sounded like," Ben said. "He was a perfectionist at that sort of thing. He could have fooled me or anyone imitating one of us. He used to do it as a private joke now and then."

"I tend to buy Chambrun's version," Herzog said after a moment of silence.

"Bully for you," Watson said. "So Pasqua goes free while you look for a dead man."

"Did March or Pasqua have some kind of rented quarters away from the Beaumont?" Herzog asked.

"When we found out that 'Mrs. Watson' was really Miss Huber," I said, "Watson said he had a room at a club down the street."

"I had a room, not Toby or Frank," Watson said. "I do have a room at the University Club. You can check with them."

"I have," Herzog said.

"Am I a suspect?"

"Anyone who is a friend of Toby March or Frank Pasqua

and has a rented room somewhere could be helping to hide a wounded man," Herzog said.

"Your room at the club has been searched," Chambrun said.

"What are you going to do to protect Mr. Chambrun?" I asked Herzog.

"He was attacked to prevent him from pushing his ideas about March," Herzog said. "By now he's pushed them as far as they can be pushed. There would be no point in being charged with another murder."

"Unless he's crazy enough to enjoy killing," Mr. White said. "After seeing my son Douglas that wouldn't surprise me a bit."

3

People began to collect in the lobby long before what would have been show time in the Blue Lagoon. Even though it had been widely announced on radio and TV that there would be no show, people were fascinated to hear something about the murders that had been suggested.

I was dead on my feet. More than twenty-four hours had passed since I'd had a touch of shut-eye. I suggested to Chambrun that I wouldn't be of much use to him unless I got a couple of hours' rest. He agreed, and told me to take off for my room. I left him with Lieutenant Herzog, Colonel Watson, and Millicent Huber and headed for my room on the second floor. I just loosened my tie and collar and lay down on top of the bed. I must have gone out like a light, because when I woke I wasn't alone, and someone was pressing something cold and hard against my forehead.

A voice with a strong foreign accent spoke.

"Do not move or cry out or you will be a dead man."

A folded cloth or handkerchief was tied around my mouth from behind and another tied over my eyes.

"We move. We go down the stairs," the accented voice said. "Most people ride elevators. Not much chance people will be walking the stairs. But if they are, they will die if they try to help you."

We walked; that cold, hard object, which I knew must be a gun, was pressed against my head. Down two floors of in-house stairs to the basement. No encounters. Then out into the fresh evening air. Surely we couldn't go down Park Avenue without being stopped. But then I realized I was being steered to the back of the building. I could hear automobile horns at a distance, but none where we walked. I was suddenly turned sharply left and down a short flight of narrow stairs, and I knew we were in the basement of a building some distance up Park Avenue from the Beaumont.

The sound of a bolt being slid open as a result of a sharp knocking by my man, and I was pushed ahead through a door. It was closed behind me and the bolt moved into a locked position again. I was pushed ahead through another door and brought to a stop. The gag and blindfold were taken from my mouth and eyes, and I found myself in a semi-dark room. Directly across from where I stood, a group of young people were huddled together. They had to be the British hostages. No one spoke a word. Then my accented captor gave me his last instructions. "You can hope your friends are more cooperative than the friends of these young people. Pray, if that's your way."

I stood there staring at the other hostages, and then one of the young men came over to me and held out his hand.

"My name is George Stewart, Jr.," he said. "You know why we're being held, and you are being held for the same reason."

"Yes. My name is Mark Haskell. I am public-relations director and general assistant to Pierre Chambrun, the general manager of the Hotel Beaumont."

Young Stewart's handshake was firm, but his hand was cold. "Two of our group have been murdered right here in this room while we were forced to watch," he said. "Frances Warren was raped and killed here. Doug White was butchered—stabbed and stabbed over and over. We couldn't lift a finger to help either of them. Men with guns deterred us. Do they explain outside why the British won't turn their prisoners free to ransom us?"

"I think I understand," I said. "Prisoners of war are a perfectly legal part of the business of war. Taking hostages isn't a legal part of anything. The British know that if they are blackmailed into freeing their prisoners of war, other hostages will be taken, other demands made. I can only tell you that everything is being done to find you, and that people who want to help are less than two city blocks away—including Douglas White's father. Scotland Yard had sent a man here, but he is dead. I suspect more are on their way."

"God, I hope they hurry," young Stewart said.

"You know that the men who are holding you are from Iran?" I asked him.

"We assume it," he said. "We have each been forced to write to a parent begging them to get Iranian prisoners freed."

"How have they treated you?"

"Does showing us brutal murders of our friends answer that?"

"Food?"

"Some cereal and milk. Nothing else."

"Sleep?"

"On the floor, if anyone could."

"The barest minimum, then."

"No more than that."

Two dark-skinned men came in from the outer room. They were each carrying a white portable telephone. One of them was holding one of the phones to his ear as if he were listening to a conversation. The other walked over to George Stewart and handed his phone to the young man. "Your father on the phone," he said. "Persuade him to get action in England or you will be next!" He passed the white phone to George, who was standing right beside me. Young Stewart held the phone a little distance away from his ear. "Dad!"

"Junior!" I could hear a frightened male voice say.

"Could you hear what this monster said to me?"

"Oh, God, I'm afraid so, boy."

"Is there any chance the government can be persuaded to do anything about the prisoners of war?"

"I'm afraid not, Junior."

"I saw what happened to Frances and Doug," George, Jr., said.

"God help us, we have seen pictures here," the father said.

"If the government won't do anything, then I have to face what's coming," young George said.

"I'd give anything if I could face it for you," his father said. "It was easier when they didn't tell us their plans."

Our jailer reached out and took the small white phone away from George, Jr. The young man cried out, "Good-bye, Dad!"

Then, suddenly, he was clinging to me.

I felt sick at my stomach. I thought I might throw up. Four dark-skinned men came into the room, each of them armed with a high-powered rifle. I was ordered to leave George and join the other young people against the far wall. The four riflemen faced us, aiming their weapons at us. One of the girls screamed. I looked away from the rifle barrel that was aimed straight at my face. The man who had handed the phone to George Stewart had thrown the young man down to the floor and had pinned him there in some kind of karate hold. He had a knife in his right hand, a full-sized carving knife. The girl behind me screamed again and I saw the most terrible violence I've ever seen. The knife was plunged into young Stewart's chest and stomach in a series of wild thrusts. Blood spurted out of the wounds. And then, as the young man opened his mouth to cry out, his throat was cut four or five times. He had to be dead. All three girls in the group were screaming at the top of their lungs now. One of the young men charged out toward Stewart's killer. One of the high-powered rifles was fired and the young man's face was obliterated.

The man who was aiming his rifle at me gestured to me to join him out on the floor. I wasn't sure my legs would hold me up but they did. He took me by the arm and led me over to the door to this basement room, and there he stopped me. From beyond the door came a new voice with a heavy British accent. Young Stewart had told me about English voices.

"You've seen what lies ahead of you, Mr. Haskell," the voice said. "We're putting you on the phone to Chambrun. He must use his contacts in Europe to get what we must have. If not, you can tell him what to expect, with you the victim."

"How much time?" I asked.

"Get him to tell us," the voice said.

The man with the little white portable phone moved me away from the door and handed the instrument to me.

"You dial your own number," he said. "The right number."

There wasn't a dial on the phone, only a series of push buttons. I punched out Chambrun's private number. He answered almost at once.

"Mark? Is that you?"

"How did you know?" I asked.

"They warned me you'd be calling. Are you all in one piece?"

"So far. You wouldn't believe what's been going on here. Another boy was murdered like Douglas White. A boy shot in the face for trying to interfere. I'm told I will be next."

"Keep your cool," Chambrun said. "I think I can get what they want for them."

I felt my heart jam against my ribs. I hadn't expected any such assurance.

"Mrs. Thatcher's government will meet about breakfast time," Chambrun said. "About four o'clock their time, ten ours."

"And they will turn over the prisoners of war for the hostages?" I asked.

"I believe they will. Feeling is running high in England."

"And do I fit into that exchange?" I asked.

"I believe you will," Chambrun said. "Tell them I'm not stalling. There isn't any way for me to move faster."

"Ten o'clock, is it?" the English voice broke into our telephone conversation.

"Ten is when they'll meet," Chambrun said. "They have to have time to discuss it, Toby."

The English voice laughed. "Still playing that game, Chambrun?"

"Who else can you be?" Chambrun said.

"You'll find out if you don't come through," the English voice said.

There was no way I could make an intelligent guess. I'd not heard Toby March speak except when he was imitating someone on stage.

"I'll do the best I can for you, Mark," Chambrun said. "Sit tight. The chances are good."

There was the clicking sound of the phone being hung up on Chambrun's end and another click of the second phone. I tried to make myself believe, but I was looking at the bloody body on the floor that had once been George Stewart, Jr.

I tried to guess who it might be Chambrun was contacting in England. He had mentioned Mrs. Thatcher's government, but I could not think of anyone in the lady's cabinet who was close to him. It suddenly occurred to me, uncomfortably, that Chambrun's conversation had been designed for the person listening on this end, the man with the British voice. It was the kind of game he might play. It might give him a few hours to do—what? Find me? How? Rescue me? How? One thing was certain. I could count on his fighting for me to the bitter end.

One of the girls who had screamed earlier was kneeling beside the boy who'd been shot. From where I was, I thought

I could see that the young man was still breathing. They were deep gasps for air. Alive but only just, I thought. I joined her. I've had quite a little first-aid experience at the Beaumont. The bullet had struck him just above his right eye and the bleeding was heavy. There had been enough bleeding at the hands of these monsters in the last hours to float a battleship. I contributed my breast-pocket handkerchief to help try to stop the flow of blood. It didn't do much for the young man.

"Who is he, in case I get to talk to the outside again?" I asked the girl.

"He's Peter Folk," the girl said. "His father is the county attorney back home. I'm Elizabeth Clark. My father is the headmaster of the local school."

The Iranians had obviously chosen victims who would matter at the home base.

"I'm afraid he doesn't stand much of a chance," I said.

"Do any of us?" the girl asked.

"My friend has just told me on the phone there's a chance the Thatcher government may be willing to make a deal."

"You believe that?" the girl asked.

"Not from what I heard before I was brought here," I said. "But the man who told me that is to be trusted farther than anyone I know. My name is Haskell, by the way, Elizabeth. Mark Haskell." I explained my job at the Beaumont and who Chambrun is.

"We were all taken prisoner back in England," the Clark girl said, "and flown here to New York in a private plane."

"You have any idea whose plane it was or where this house is?"

"Neither," the girl answered. "The people who took us

prisoner all spoke with an accent, like the one you've heard here. Most of them didn't speak English at all. Douglas White, who was killed when we got here, just like poor George Stewart, said they were from the Middle East somewhere. His father has some connection with the diplomatic corps in England. Douglas spoke a smattering of several languages. He recognized the Iranian language."

"That's the story here in New York," I said. "But the English voices you've been hearing here — were they on the plane that brought you here?"

"I didn't hear them until we were brought here," Elizabeth said.

"Are they familiar to you from any other place in your past?" I asked.

"No. I never heard them before."

"Have you done very much flying in your time? Do you know what kind of plane brought you here?"

"I have no idea, as I've told you."

"Let's go to English accents like yours," I said. "In my country, you can sometimes tell the city people come from by their accents. Certainly what part of the country they come from."

"And you have got a big country compared to ours," the girl said.

"So maybe I'm exaggerating just a little," I said. "Tell me, were you involved in hiring Toby March to sing at your fair?"

"We all were," Elizabeth said. "That's how we all came to be together when these people took us."

"Took you from where?" I asked.

"The fairgrounds in Farmington. A couple of people we knew recommended Toby March to us for our fair."

"A couple of people? Local people?"

Elizabeth nodded. "Millicent Huber. She had been his nurse. And a Colonel Watson who was an orderly at the hospital. They'd attended this Toby March after a face-disfiguring accident."

"The hospital?"

"Yes. They said he was pretty spectacular. They decribed his act. They said he could imitate anyone, singing or talking."

"But you hired him to sing?"

Elizabeth nodded. "Talking didn't sound like much fun to us. But when we walked into the rehearsal hall, Toby was there along with Millicent — who, by the way, went to school with my mother. Toby was wearing a black mask. 'My name is Laurence Olivier,' he said. And then he did a piece of dialogue from Olivier's most recent film. He needn't have told us who he was. He was unmistakable."

"That good?"

"That wasn't all. He switched after a little while to Errol Flynn. We actually applauded him. Then March went over to the piano and sat down at the keyboard. He played wonderfully well — and sang. It was Frank Sinatra. No mistaking it. The voice. The musical technique. Walk into the room and you would swear it was Sinatra."

"Even with the mask on?"

"Even with it on. After a little while, he did some Crosby for us and Tony Bennett's San Francisco number."

"And then when you discussed business with him?" I asked.

"He never discussed anything with us without the mask.

'It would spoil the performance for you,' he told us. 'You would be seeing me when I recreated somebody else for you.'

"Anyway, we didn't discuss business for very long. He was asking too much. We went home raving about him. Doug White's father heard our enthusiasm and announced he would go to hear Toby for himself. He came back completely sold. He put up the money."

"But March did talk to you as himself. You would know the sound of his voice if you heard it again?" I asked.

"I don't think so," Elizabeth said. "He was Laurence Olivier all the way down the road."

"So you couldn't identify him if you ever saw him again?"

"No way possible. He wants it that way. Of course, the people involved with him, the supporting musicians, and his manager, whose name I think is Pasqua, might."

"You would know them?"

Elizabeth gave me a shy smile. "I dated one of the musicians named Ben Lewis," she said. "They played at the fair for a week, and I went out with Ben at least four times."

"Did he talk to you at all about March and Pasqua?"

"Ben is quite a musician," the girl said. "He plays several instruments. The one he is primarily hired to play is the guitar. But that is one of Toby March's specialties, too, so Ben doesn't get written into the score too often with it. But he is a tremendous admirer of March's. He doesn't feel cheated out of playing his best instrument. As a matter of fact, he says March has helped him enormously and that he owes him for that."

"Am I right in guessing that March is some kind of a musical hero to those young men who play for him?"

"You've never heard him play?"

"Just this last Saturday night," I said. "I thought he was pretty marvelous."

"Oh yes. They think he's tops. But all of them think highly of each other, and particularly the man who is their agent and public-relations man."

"Frank Pasqua?"

"A lovely man," the girl said, her face warming. "Has something happened to him? Before Doug White was killed, he heard something on the radio in the next room. It said that Toby March and Frank were both missing."

"That's the way it is," I told her.

"They would seem to be much more important as hostages than our group. I suppose our parents —?"

"Mr. Chambrun hopes he can get your Mrs. Thatcher to give in to some extent to your jailers."

"I don't think she will," Elizabeth said. "She's a tough old girl. It wouldn't be like her to let herself be blackmailed."

"That's the general public's feeling," I said. "But I need to ask you something quite personal, Elizabeth. Did you ever have a date with Frank Pasqua? What might be called 'unfinished business.'"

She flushed. "Well, he was a very attractive man, Mark. When the show was over in the evening at the fair, Toby March and the musicians left. Frank stayed at the fairgrounds. He bought me a few drinks. But there was nothing 'unfinished.'"

"Last night? Saturday night?"

"For God's sake, Mark, all of us were prisoners, here in this place. We were flown over from England days ago. None of us ever set an unmolested foot on United States soil."

"Why do you suppose you were brought here?" I asked.

"Where could we be more safely hidden? I don't understand, Mark, why my country, Great Britain, should be holding Iranian prisoners of war. We're not at war."

"Persian Gulf," I suggested. "All the Western allies are involved there."

"But Iran wouldn't expect special favors from your government, would they? Favors that would help her hold us hostage here?"

"It's hard to believe. None of it makes very much sense."

The girl's face twisted and twitched. She was looking at the two dead boys just beyond us. "It's not children's games," she said.

The hostages, eight of us now including me, were all crowded into one corner of the room, watched over by four jailers who gabbled at each other in a foreign language I'd never heard before. Their guns were in their belts, always ready, and the way they looked at us told us clearly that they had no affection for us!

Suddenly there was a smashing sound from behind us. I spun around to see a small army burst into the room. It was headed by Chambrun, armed with a pistol, flanked on his left by Jerry Dodd, and on his right by Lieutenant Herzog and Colonel Watson. Each of them had a gun leveled at one of the jailers. Behind them were about a dozen uniformed, armed cops.

Watson was yelling something at the top of his lungs in the same strange language the jailers had been using. The jailers seemed frozen where they stood. None of them reached for his gun, and they were all focused on Watson, who kept shouting at them. Eventually, very reluctantly, the jailers pulled their guns out of their belts and dropped them on the floor. Instantly, the armed cops charged them and handcuffed them.

Chambrun turned to me. "Miracles by the score," he said.

My voice was so unsteady I scarcely recognized it myself. "How did you find us?" I asked him.

"They outsmarted themselves," Chambrun said. "When they phoned us to say you were going to call, we got organized. Herzog alerted the phone company, and when you did call, they were able to trace the phone you were using to this house."

Chambrun turned and called out, "Okay, Doc, come on in!"

Doctor Partridge came in from the outer room followed by a half dozen of the hotel's bellhops bringing in stretchers on wheels.

"Any of these youngsters hurt?" Chambrun asked.

"The two out there on the floor are beyond help, I'm afraid." I was referring to the Stewart boy who had been butchered and the Folk boy who'd been shot. "I wouldn't have minded if you had shot down those creeps."

"Second miracle," Chambrun said. "If those jailers had moved around and threatened us, we couldn't have fired. I'd probably have nailed you." He looked down at his pistol. "I'm not an expert with this thing. They didn't know it but they had us behind the eight ball if they hadn't obeyed Watson's instructions."

The bellhops were loading the two dead young men onto stretchers. "Anyone here hurt?" Chambrun called out to the almost dazed hostages. No one spoke. "We'll get you back to the hotel where we'll keep you safe."

"How did Watson know how to speak to them?" I asked.

"It seems he was attached to the British embassy in Lebanon at one time. He knows the language well. He volunteered, and we had sense enough to accept his offer of help. There's a lot more. We have a new man from Scotland Yard at the hotel. It wasn't prisoners of war they were after, but money. Three million dollars for whoever of the hostages is left alive."

"So the game isn't over?" I asked.

"Unless they quit, which I doubt. It'll be money and these four men we just took."

Two of the girls were clinging together, weeping. The boys, apparently stunned, were watching Doc Partridge remove their dead friends. Chambrun went on talking in his clear, sharp voice.

"Douglas White's father is here, along with the new Scotland Yard man, Inspector Stanwyck. You'll be able to talk to your families in England, and should be on your way home before the end of the day."

"Bless you, Mr. Chambrun," Elizabeth Clark said.

"I'm sorry we weren't in time for all of you," Chambrun said, watching the last stretcher with its load of death being wheeled out of the room. "There isn't much point in trying to hide your walk to the hotel. It's only a couple of blocks. Whoever may be watching will know that the Beaumont is an impenetrable fortress."

The plan was already made. Chambrun had decided the hostages should occupy the second penthouse on the roof, the one located between his and Victoria Haven's. There was no way of getting up to the roof except by elevator or the emergency fire escape, both of which could be covered like a tent by guards.

Crowds we had, like 'em or not. The sidewalks outside the brownstone where we'd been held were jammed, and a cheer that sounded like something from a football stadium rocked the neighborhood. I walked beside Chambrun at the head of the column, which was surrounded by Herzog and his men.

"I still don't believe what I saw," I said. "The butchering of that Stewart boy was a nightmare you couldn't have invented."

Herzog had stationed men outside the Beaumont so that there was a way for us to talk through the crowd to get inside. It felt like getting home to walk into the lobby. We went directly to the two elevators that would take us to the roof and the penthouses.

The middle penthouse is normally reserved for very special guests, and I suspect that the young people who were taken there were about as special as you can get.

Waiting for us inside was Mr. White and a stern-looking older man with close-cropped white hair who turned out to be Scotland Yard's Inspector Stanwyck.

Mr. White, of course, knew all the young people. They had been his son's close friends. They greeted him as though he were family.

"I can't begin to pass on all the messages I have for you," he managed to say. He was looking around as though someone was missing. We had grim news for him and Chambrun told him what it was.

120

"I'm afraid we have messages for home that aren't so cheerful," he said. "The terrorists have killed two more of this group, George Stewart, Jr., and the Folk boy."

"Oh my God," Mr. White said, and covered his face with his hands for a moment. "We have taken four of them prisoner, and it's possible we can get them to talk. Not in general, I hope."

"I'm afraid that may be an optimistic outlook," Colonel Watson said. He had come with us up to the penthouse. "These Iranians view their terrorism as a kind of religion. No kind of counterviolence will loosen their tongues. They will die before they give you the smallest clue to their leader. If that would do you any good."

Mr. White lowered his hands from his ash-gray face. "I'd better get on the phone to George Stewart and Jeremy Folk," he said. "It may be easier for them coming from me than from a stranger."

"If there is any way to make it easier," Chambrun said, "tell them it was brutal but quick. There's a phone in the bedroom over there."

Mr. White left us and I was standing alone with Chambrun and Inspector Stanwyck. Chambrun spoke to the young people. "Miss Ruysdale is ordering food and drink for you from room service. It will be served to you here in a very few minutes."

"I'm afraid Colonel Watson is right," Stanwyck said. "The men you arrested aren't going to talk, no matter what kind of pressure you put on them. As I understand it, Mr. Chambrun, two of your people are still not accounted for — Toby March and his public-relations man, Frank Pasqua."

"Not accounted for," Chambrun said, "and with no leads to follow."

"You had a theory that one of them might be behind all this?" Stanwyck asked.

"One of them was badly wounded and would have needed help to get away," Chambrun said. "Of course, our security people were not looking for major violence at that time. Pasqua had been seen going to his room; later, March to his. It wasn't until the next afternoon when the maid went to those rooms to clean and make the beds that the evidence of a bloody struggle was discovered. The two men were gone. Security had not seen anyone leave. But they could have waited hours after they were seen going into their rooms before trying to leave. They were being watched to protect them from goggle-eyed fans, not killers."

"But you heard from Pasqua—a phone call?"

"After the news had broken on radio and TV," Chambrun said. "Mark took the call, thought he recognized Pasqua's voice. Pasqua was sure March could take care of himself, and he had 'unfinished business' to take care of."

Stanwyck looked at me. "You recognized the voice, Mr. Haskell? You knew him well enough to be sure of the voice?"

I shrugged. "I'd done all the booking busines with him, an hour or more of business dealings. It sounded like him. I had no reason at that time to doubt that it was."

"But—?"

"Mr. Chambrun pointed out that March is a genius at imitating voices. In other words, there were two people out there who could sound like Pasqua. The man himself and Toby March."

"And you think now—?"

"That it could have been either one. But I have no basis on which to make a choice."

"I can tell you one thing, Inspector," Colonel Watson broke in, "Toby could never in this world be responsible for the horrors that have gone on. He is a gentle and compassionate man."

"And any evidence to make your theory stick, Mr. Chambrun?" Stanwyck asked.

"A strong hunch," Chambrun said.

"The house where you found these young people—did you search there for March and Pasqua?"

"Herzog's men are taking it apart now, brick by brick," Chambrun said. "If they find anything, we'll know instantly."

"At Scotland Yard, we don't have a technique for handling hunches," Stanwyck said. "Do you have a hunch as to where these two men may be hiding?"

"No. Hunches don't come in bunches, Inspector."

"I understand there is a woman who is Toby March's love," Stanwyck said.

"Millicent Huber. You want to talk to her? You think you can find her, Colonel?"

Watson nodded and headed for the door.

Stanwyck called after him, "With her hackles down, please."

In the doorway, Watson passed a room-service crew bringing an elaborate buffet for the hostages. There was chicken, roast beef, salads, coffee, some bottles of white wine. Even young people in shock couldn't resist it. We learned they'd had practically nothing to eat for more than a day. Mr. White came back from the bedroom where he'd been phoning to England.

"You could probably hear the shouts of joy if you were still," he said. "Except, of course, for the Stewarts and the Folks. God, I hated to have to tell them!"

"Better you than anyone else," Chambrun said, "because they know you know how they're feeling."

Watson came back with Millicent Huber in tow. She must have been close by for him to find her so quickly.

"I'd like to talk to Miss Huber alone," Stanwyck said. "Nothing secret. It may be easier to talk about her friend without strangers listening."

"I'm his friend and she knows it," Watson said.

"We've already questioned Miss Huber," Chambrun said. "I doubt if she will have anything new to us to tell you."

Stanwyck shrugged. He indicated a comfortable armchair to Millicent. In the background, the young people were expressing delight with their food.

"As I understand it, you met Toby March at St. Elmo's hospital in London," Stanwyck began.

"I was a nurse there," Millicent said. "He was brought in for plastic surgery following an accident that destroyed his face."

"How successful was the operation?"

"That's a hard question to answer, Inspector. I never saw him before the accident."

"Would you know him if you ran into him on the street now without his mask?"

"Probably not, unless he spoke to me. I'd know his voice anywhere."

"English accent?"

"He has what I'd call a 'cultivated' way of speaking," Millicent said. "I suppose it would sound British to most people."

Stanwyck turned to Chambrun. "Could his voice have been the 'English voice' the hostages heard in the next room in the house where you found them?"

"Any voice they heard could have been his, because he could make himself sound like anyone he wanted to imitate," Chambrun said.

"Did he learn this imitation act he does while he was in the hospital?" Stanwyck asked the lady.

"I think you could say he perfected it there," Millicent said. "He'd always been in show business. He was embarrassed about how he looked after his operation. He had to find a way he could perform without revealing his ugly scars and wounds. I—I bought him his first mask. At that time his face was still badly scarred—"

"And you, Colonel Watson, you knew him then?"

Watson nodded. "I was an orderly at the time. Toby did his act for me. A collection of songs by Frank Sinatra. They were great, particularly after Millicent bought the mask for him."

"But you saw his face before he wore the mask?"

"Not really. It was all bandages and tape. You asked Millicent if she'd know him if she met him on the street. I know I would not, without the mask."

"What this adds up to is that he could have walked out of 17C after the violence there last night and no one would have known him?"

"That's the way it is, Inspector," Watson replied.

"Where did March go with his act, after he was released from the hospital?" Stanwyck asked Millicent.

"All over England, Europe."

"You had become his lover by then? You traveled with him?"

"Not always. He was trying to put together the little group of musicians who are now with him. The first time around the circuit, I didn't go with him. The second time, I went with him. What we called home was London."

"Where did the circuit cover?"

"France, Italy, West Germany, Belgium, Holland, Spain. I may have left some place out."

"Iran?" Stanwyck asked.

"I don't recall him mentioning Iran."

"Or the Ayatollah Khomeini?"

"Of course Iran and the Ayatollah were front-page news for a number of years. I can't say Toby never mentioned him, but he certainly never mentioned taking his act to Iran."

"Did he speak foreign languages?"

"Smatterings," Millicent said. "The way most of us do when we move around. 'Where is the bathroom? A cup of coffee, please. A telephone?' Things like that."

"But he wasn't fluent in any other language but English?"

"Not that I ever heard."

Stanwyck spread his hands. "Thanks for your help, Miss Huber. Unfortunately we don't seem any closer to anything useful than we were before."

"When did the money come into the picture?" Chambrun asked. "We hadn't heard of it before your arrival, Inspector."

126

"It's always been there," Stanwyck said. "Three million dollars in British pounds."

"Why British pounds?"

"I suppose they plan to spend it somewhere in the Empire," Stanwyck said.

"Has it been raised?" Chambrun asked, looking at Douglas White's father.

"The families of these young people aren't rich," he said.

"They don't need to be rich," Chambrun said. "The government would surely help them. In this country you could raise it in ten-dollar bills through the mail before breakfast!"

"Nobody wants to see these bastards make a profit from our young people," Mr. White said.

"Do they want to see them dead, cut into small pieces?" Chambrun's face was stony.

Mr. White's mouth twitched. "I suppose it can and will be raised." He squared his shoulders. "I wish I'd been with you when you rescued the hostages! I'd have killed the first guard I could have laid hands on."

"That's why you weren't invited," Chambrun said. "That kind of move might have killed all of the hostages."

Jerry Dodd came into the room. He was carrying a large-sized business envelope. "Certified mail for you, boss, care of Colonel Watson."

"Why on earth?" Watson asked.

"Because you can read their bloody language," Chambrun said. "Open it and read it."

Watson opened the letter and took out a couple of large sheets of paper. His lips moved as he glanced at it. Then he squared his shoulders and began to read.

Chambrun:

Since you insist on getting into the game, you have now become the principal player. I've directed this to your loud-mouthed British colonel because he can read it to you.

"Iranian?" Chambrun asked.
Colonel Watson nodded and went on reading.

I suppose the British will arrange to fly the kids home. They don't matter any longer.

"Thank God!" Mr. White muttered.

But the games goes on. You will raise three million dollars, Chambrun, in British pounds. You will have it on hand by an hour after the banks open tomorrow morning. You will turn it over to one of the four men you arrested a while ago. You will turn all four of them loose. They will know where to bring the money. Don't have them followed or I give you my word you and your hotel will be blown into the East River. And I am a man who keeps his word. Wednesday morning at ten o'clock is your deadline. Get moving, Mr. Wise Guy.

That was apparently the end of it.
"Signed?" Chambrun asked.
" 'Your executioner,' " Watson read.
"Can you do it?" Mr. White asked.

"Your question should be 'Will I do it?' " Chambrun said.

"Well?" Mr. White asked.

"It will depend on what happens to these young people," Chambrun said. "Have arrangements been made to get them back to England?"

"There are two British air-force planes waiting at the airport to fly them home," Inspector Stanwyck said.

"So move them," Chambrun said. "When we know they are safe with their people, we'll decide how to respond to this threat."

"While they're being flown to England, there should be time to raise the money," Mr. White said, "if that's what you plan to do."

"I would expect you and their families to help with that," Chambrun said. "These aren't American children, and the response here might not be as spontaneous as if they were."

" 'Blow you and your hotel into the East River' was a pretty wild threat. And yet—" Mr. White said.

"They could have planted bombs God knows how long ago," Jerry Dodd said.

"You know better than anyone how hard it will be to find them," Chambrun said. "Five hundred rooms. Thousands of bureau drawers, closets, and shoe boxes. It will take a week to cover every kind of hiding place."

"We could get lucky," Jerry said.

"You want your life to depend on that kind of luck?" Chambrun asked.

"You know how little they care for human life," Watson said. "No more for property."

"Or how little the general public cares about my life or the Beaumont building," Chambrun said.

"You could refuse to play along," Jerry said.

"Tell me how, Jerry. I'm not ready to die. Are you, or will you and your people desert me and not search for bombs?"

"Surely the police—" Inspector Stanwyck said.

"The police, the FBI, the CIA," Chambrun said, "but none of them would be worth a damn searching this hotel."

"You know we won't quit on you, Mr. Chambrun," Jerry Dodd said. "The whole damned hotel force will volunteer to help. You know that."

"I'd like to think so," Chambrun said.

"You may be overlooking your best bet," Inspector Stanwyck said. "Somewhere here in America there must be someone who is important to Iran. That person might be a worthwhile counter-hostage."

"The first thing," Chambrun said, "is to get these young people on their way home so that they're no longer a part of it. I'd like to think that there is a payoff for at least one action I've taken today."

"I'll get in touch with Washington," Inspector Stanwyck said. "They are supposed to be sending men to guard and transport the kids."

No one had asked me if I'd stay here and stand by my boss. I knew I would, of course, but what I didn't know was how helpful I could be.

"There are crowds of curious people milling about in your hotel, Mr. Chambrun," Watson said. "I'd love to go and mingle among them. If any of those Iranian jerks are there, I'll bet I could smell 'em!"

Chambrun made an impatient gesture suggesting Watson should leave, and he did.

"We had better set up some kind of security to guard you, Mr. Chambrun," Jerry Dodd said.

Chambrun gave him a bitter smile. "I should be perfectly safe until ten o'clock tomorrow morning—an hour after the banks open. Who knows, I might be cooking up three million dollars for them. I should be safe until I've failed!"

4

The next hour in the penthouses, most of the attention was focused on the young British people. There were overseas phone calls from relieved parents. There were official instructions for Inspector Stanwyck from British officials. The readiness of two British air-force planes was confirmed. Young Miss Elizabeth Clark came over to stand by me.

"Thanks, Mr. Haskell, for helping me to stay in one piece," she said.

"I'm the one who's going to need help now," I said.

"Mr. Chambrun looks able to take care of himself," she said.

"They just missed shooting him in the head a while back," I said. "It could happen again."

"While he's trying to raise money for them?" the girl asked.

I wished I could convince myself. If these young people got back to England safely, Chambrun would be responsible. The terrorists might make him pay for that, money or no money. I turned to Lieutenant Herzog, who was watching the British air-force people come in from the roof to take the former hostages.

"Will there be any problem turning loose the four Iranians you arrested this morning?" I asked him.

"It won't be routine," Herzog said, "considering the possible murder of many hotel guests."

"I suspect Chambrun will have evacuated all the guests before the payoff time comes," I said. "It will be up to you to deal with hundreds of sightseers."

I left Penthouse Two and walked over to Chambrun's quarters. I had expected him to be busy on the phone, calling friends who might help him with the money problem. Instead, he was in the kitchen making himself a pot of coffee.

"You have to have something to keep going," he said. "Care to join me?"

I nodded. I glanced at the Mr. Coffee machine and saw that it was nearly finished brewing. Suddenly I wanted some badly.

"Thanks for not taking off, Mark," Chambrun said.

"You didn't think I would, did you?"

"You witnessed an unthinkable scene," he said, "that could be enough to send any man on his way. You also know that I'm not likely to let those bastards get what they want."

"And so?" I asked.

"And so we have twelve hours in which to nail them to a cross," Chambrun said.

"How, if you don't know where to find them or who they are?"

"I don't have any doubt at all that the man we want is Toby March," Chambrun said. "With or without the help of Frank Pasqua."

"You're convinced of that without a shred of proof?" I asked.

"How much proof do you need?"

"Maybe they are being held as hostages," I said.

"Then why haven't we been asked to pay something or put up something for their release?" Chambrun asked.

"You might be expected to do more to save your own neck and your own property than anyone else's," I said.

"Then why involve themselves with other prisoners? Why not attack us directly?" Chambrun asked. "They don't dare suggest freeing Toby March or Frank Pasqua in return for money. The British kids were perfect. Now that they're free, only my property and my life are enough to force me to get them what they want."

"Money and the hotel?"

"What else would move me?" Chambrun asked.

"So you will raise the money and set your prisoners free?" I asked.

"I will make it look as though I plan to do that," Chambrun said, "but I hope to nail them before payoff time arrives."

"But, boss, you could find yourself talking to him in the lobby or at one of the bars, and you wouldn't know it was him," I said. "Even the woman who lives with him and the old friend, Colonel Watson, can't tell you what he looks like."

"Or what he sounds like," Chambrun said. "No one has ever described his speech pattern, as if he has no distinguishable one of his own."

"He must have spoken in his own voice in bed with Millicent!"

"He was hiding from her as well as everyone else."

"A strange compulsion," I said.

"Cutting people up into small pieces is a little strange, too, don't you think?" Chambrun asked.

"So you are behind a pretty large eight ball," I said.

Chambrun opened his jacket, and I saw that he was wearing a shoulder holster with his pistol there. "I never before prepared to kill a man," Chambrun said. "This bastard is different."

"Do that and his Iranian friends will carry out his threats," I said.

"We'll have an army waiting for them," Chambrun said.

Where do we go from here, I wondered.

The coffee machine had finished brewing, and Chambrun poured us each a mug of rich, black coffee. He took a swallow of his and headed for the living room. There he went directly to his desk, where, with a key from a ring of keys he carried in his pocket, he opened the top drawer. From it he produced another gun, and he held it out to me. I shied away as if it were a rattlesnake.

"I want you to shadow me, Mark," Chambrun said. "You see anyone make any kind of a move toward me that looks threatening, use this."

"I honestly don't think I could," I said. My mouth felt dry. "I don't think I could shoot at a man to kill, even if you were threatened."

"I don't want you to kill anyone," Chambrun said. "Just fire this gun in the air, toward the ceiling. That will throw whoever it is off base and alert me. I'm surprised, though. You did see the Stewart boy killed. That you could feel pity—"

"I wouldn't be feeling pity," I said. "I just wouldn't trust myself to hit the broadside of a barn with this gun. I've never used one in my life."

"Only I will know that when you fire it," Chambrun said. "Now, I'm going to get in touch with George Boswell at the bank. If we have to raise three million bucks, I'll need his help. I can't spend the day calling my friends on the phone."

"You're thinking of paying?" I asked.

"If it's the only answer," he said. "It is going to be hell around here, Mark. March and his friends will know whether I'm making any kind of a move to raise the money. If I don't go through the motions, he may not wait until his deadline."

"There's still no doubt in your mind that it's March?" I asked.

"Come up with someone else."

"Pasqua," I said.

"That's a team, March and Pasqua," Chambrun said.

"It's hard to believe—"

"Even split two ways, three million dollars is a lot of money." Chambrun picked up the phone, dialed a number, and asked for George Boswell when someone answered. It was a pretty wild story when you heard Chambrun tell it. The bloody details were something out of a horror movie.

"I've got to get fifteen hundred people, guests and staff, out of the hotel before the end of the day," Chambrun told his banker. "I know—I know—"

Chambrun put down the phone. "The money isn't impossible," he said to me. "But getting people to leave the Beaumont may be something else. A lot of them will be decent enough to want to stand by me."

"Especially the staff," I said.

"The average man in the street hates terrorism," Chambrun said. "Even though they aren't personal friends, many of the hotel guests may want to help us face it in a strong way."

"It might be helpful, mightn't it?" I asked. "There could be a thousand people shadowing you, not just me."

"How many deaths do you think I want on my conscience?" Chambrun asked.

It turned out not to be something that could be accomplished just by asking or ordering. The people in the hotel had a little less than twelve hours before the deadline. In that time they might be able to do something to help Chambrun, who had always been a friend. We suddenly knew how they felt when we went down into the lobby. At the sight of Chambrun there were cheers, shouts of friendship and reassurance. It was heartwarming. People crowded around him, promising to stand by. I suddenly realized there was one disadvantage in this. If a terrorist was in the crowd, I'd never be able to spot him soon enough to fire a warning shot! It was Chambrun who brought some kind of order to the situation. He stood up on a chair and waved his arms for silence. He got it.

"I can't tell you how grateful I am for your support," he called out to them. "I'm not asking you to leave primarily to save your own lives. But there are so many of you, my dear friends, and the monsters who are out to get me and destroy my hotel can move in a crowd without attracting attention. They would become just part of you and your so-much-appreciated friendship. If you would simply leave the hotel unoccupied except by the police and me, then they can't act unnoticed. We would have a chance to catch them that way. So I ask you, please, pack your luggage and go. I promise you, when this is all over, we will stage a party here for all of you the likes of which have never been seen before. Please, please go and give us our best chance."

He was applauded again, and then a man whom I recognized as the owner of a big department store in the area took over.

"I think we should do as Mr. Chambrun asks. It makes sense, and it could be safer for him. We'll give you the party when the time comes, Mr. Chambrun."

Chambrun raised his arms again. "I'm grateful," he said, "and I love you all."

The crowd started to break up, but he called out to them once more. "When you are packing your belongings, if you see anything in a bureau drawer or a closet that doesn't belong to you, don't touch it or handle it. It could be an explosive or something that would set off an explosive."

There was a murmur of voices as people left.

In all the years that I have worked for Chambrun at the Beaumont, I've never seen the place empty. Oh, in the dawn hours, when the bars and clubs are closed, there is no human traffic, but you know, instinctively, that hundreds and hundreds of guests are in the rooms overhead and surrounding you. Suddenly it was different. People were scurrying out, only a few bellboys to help them. So many people had never left at one time before.

Chambrun and I stood near the front revolving door, he

speaking occasionally to an acquaintance. I knew a lot of them by sight and who they were, but they were not *my* friends.

Chambrun glanced at his wristwatch. "Still take another hour," he said. "It is hard to remember how long it takes a man to put a clean shirt in a suitcase."

Colonel Watson approached us from the elevator. Millicent Huber was with him.

"I assume you aren't including us in your exit orders," he said. "After all, I'm a professional at this kind of situation, and I speak the enemy's language in case you need to communicate with them."

"No, I don't want you to go, Colonel," Chambrun said.

"Any luck with the money?" Watson asked.

"Let me say I'm optimistic."

"Not many men could come up with that kind of answer," Watson said. "Friends that wealthy don't grow on vines."

"I have helped a lot of people in different ways over the years," Chambrun said. "They don't seem to be shocked when I ask for help in return."

Watson shook his head. "I don't suppose you have been watching television or listening to a radio. The coverage is almost as constant, complete, and sympathetic to you as it was for that little girl who fell down a well in Texas some time back. People who never heard of you until today seem to want to be helpful."

"I take it you haven't 'smelled' the enemy," Chambrun said.

"Not so far. But I suspect they'll stay out of sight until the time for dealing gets closer."

"Well, thanks for *your* help," Chambrun said. "It may save the day when crisis time comes."

"I hope so," Watson said.

"You say you are a professional at this kind of situation. Meaning —?"

"Terrorism," Watson said. "It's a way of life in Iran."

"So you can make a good guess as to what to expect?"

"I'd say you are a way station," Watson said. "You are a potential means for raising the money they need."

"Money they need for what?"

"Buying missiles from the Chinese and others," Watson said.

"To use against whom?"

"The Western world in the Persian Gulf," Watson said, "and the Iraqis, with whom they've been at war for years, and the Russians, when they think they can get away with it. Money is the name of the game. They don't hate you, Chambrun, or your hotel. They just want to force you to raise the cash for them that they need to proceed."

"So that is why they butchered those British kids?"

Watson shook his head, slowly. "The British aren't as casual about money as you are here in this country. But their children!"

"But they haven't raised the money to save their kids," Chambrun said.

"The parents don't have it. They have to talk someone out of it. You look like an easier mark to them. You will do almost anything to save your property. The hotel."

Chambrun's smile was bitter. "And so I will," he said.

Jerry Dodd joined us. "People are starting to move out," he said, "bag and baggage. No one has reported finding anything suspicious. I'm sending a man into each room as it is

140

vacated to look for anything unusual. So far nothing has been reported or found."

"I suggest you concentrate on this upper level," Watson said. "Chambrun and these penthouses, visible from all over the city, are their most likely targets."

"No one is getting within three floors of this top level," Jerry said. "My men have already covered the elevators, the fire stairs, and any other way up. Clean as a whistle. Stay up here, Mr. Chambrun, and you will be safe."

Chambrun reached out and touched Jerry's arm. "Have you seen Betsy anywhere? I haven't seen her since that mob scene downstairs when I told the people to leave the hotel."

Betsy Ruysdale, I knew, was the closest person in the world to his heart. If she were threatened, it would change his whole approach to the problem.

"I want her with me," Chambrun said to Jerry.

"I'll do my best," Jerry said. "I just wanted you to know that things are under way." He turned and left us.

"Miss Ruysdale is special to you?" Watson asked.

"Best executive secretary in the world," Chambrun said, and turned to me. "See if you can help Jerry find her, Mark."

I hesitated and looked up at the ceiling. My right hand was closed over the gun in my jacket pocket. Chambrun read the message. "Betsy comes first," he said.

"You have any idea where she might be involved?" I asked him.

"She was going to help Atterbury at the front desk," he said, "with the hundreds of people checking out, wanting to leave messages, addresses where they might be going, phone numbers, and the like.

"She was there when I came up here. She planned to stay until the night crew could be given an emergency call. They all live outside of the hotel, as you know. She told me she'd be right up to the nest when they reported."

"The nest?"

He smiled at me. "Betsy and I call this penthouse 'The Bird's Nest,'" he said. "Maybe she couldn't get past Jerry's men, though they know her and that she belongs here with me."

"Do my best," I said. I patted my pocket. "You stay here until I get back."

I had no trouble getting down to the lobby. Jerry's men were not stopping anyone from leaving the upper floors. Atterbury, the chief desk clerk, looked half dead when I got down to his station at the front desk. The crowd in the lobby had thinned out, but there must have been at least a hundred people still waiting to be checked out.

I let myself in the back way, and Atterbury gave me a grateful look. "The night crew is supposed to report," he said, "but they must have died on the way. Not a joke, man. Betsy was supposed to call them in, but she took off."

"Where to?"

"No idea. She called out to me that she'd be back in a few minutes. She's never shown."

"You don't know where she went?"

"With some woman," Atterbury said. "I looked up a few minutes after she told me she had to go somewhere, and saw her walking toward the main door with a woman."

"Someone you know?"

He shook his head. "About half the world was here in the

lobby then. Their backs were to me. I recognized Betsy's bright blue dress, but the dame with her drew a blank. Tall-ish, dark hair worn long in the back. But I never saw her face. It didn't matter then. Betsy had said she would be back in a moment, and Betsy does what she says she will do. But not this time." He turned away. "We'll be buried here if I don't take care of this mob."

It was true. People were shouting for attention. Cham-brun was right. He'd gotten their attention, but he'd also managed to spread panic in the ranks.

It wasn't pleasant to think of Betsy and the English girl who had been raped and beaten to death in the same thought, but I could not escape it. I couldn't find one of Jerry's men or anyone else on the staff who had seen Betsy leaving with a woman.

I was just about to leave the desk to mingle out on the floor, just in case someone had seen Betsy and her companion, when someone grabbed my arm. It was an unsteady grip. I looked down. It was Maggie Hanson, Frank Pasqua's lady. Her red hair was disheveled. The oilskin slicker she was wear-ing didn't do anything for her sexy figure.

"Any news?" she asked.

"About Frank? Not a whisper."

"Oh, my God," she said.

"Either he or Toby March called me on the phone," I said. "The police are trying to find out who that call came from."

"But you said it was Frank! You recognized his voice."

"There is a theory that it might have been Toby imitating Frank."

"Why on earth?"

"To throw us off," I said. "Somewhere here in New York, both Toby and Frank must each have had more than one good friend. We need to find those friends, Maggie."

"You don't understand," Maggie said. "For more than a year now they've been playing different cities all over the world. You don't settle down to close friendships when you are on that kind of roller coaster."

"But Toby is famous now. People everywhere must be trying to get their hooks into him. The best way to reach him is through his close friend and associate, Frank."

"The important thing is the press," Maggie said. "You don't have to send for them. They are in your hair the minute you hit town. They are in your hair from the very first."

"Is there any one reporter who is close to Frank?" I asked.

"Jack Denny. He is the entertainment editor for *Nightlife Magazine*. I understand they once worked together on a midwestern newspaper."

"Let's see if we can get in touch with Denny at *Nightlife*," I suggested. I pulled Maggie into the registration booth and asked information for *Nightlife*'s number. There was a prompt answer when I dialed the number given to me. I asked for Denny. There was no eagerness to connect me with him until I identified myself as the public-relations man for the Beaumont. A moment later, I was talking to Jack Denny.

"Frank and I used to work together in Cleveland," he told me. "I have been listening to the radio and watching television for hours. What's going on, Haskell?"

"I hoped you could tell us," I said.

"Frank called me before the show went on at the Beaumont," Denny said. "We made a date to get together today. I've been wondering if he'll keep the date."

"Wait for him," I said. "If he shows, hang onto him until I get there. Tell him I'm bringing his girl with me. Where are you to meet?"

"The Spartan Bar."

"I can be there in five minutes," I said.

"It will take me nearer a half hour," Denny said. "I'm on my way."

I guess I don't have to say that Pasqua didn't show up for their meeting.

Karl Nevers, the headwaiter at the Spartan Bar, knew Jack Denny as an old and friendly customer. "He holds many of his interviews here," Karl told me.

"Is there a table reserved for him?"

"Yes. Jack Denny reserved a table and told me a Mr. Pasqua was to be his guest."

Maggie Hanson and I waited at a corner table for the reporter. He was as good as his word—a little less than half an hour had passed when Karl brought him over to the table.

"I wasn't coming," Denny said, "after what I'd heard on the radio. I knew Frank wasn't going to show, whatever his problem is."

Denny was a slender, athletic-looking man with an attractive suntan. He looked about forty, I guessed. I introduced him to Maggie.

"When did Pasqua make his lunch date with you for today?" I asked him.

"Some time before Saturday night's performance."

"You cover pop music for your magazine?" I asked. "Like every other reporter in the field, you must be curious about Toby March—what he really looks like."

Denny grinned. "I tried to catch him off base a dozen times," he said, "but he plays his game behind that mask really close. I never came near getting an unguarded look at him."

I couldn't tell him Chambrun's theory about March. It was his story to reveal when he chose.

"When Pasqua called you to make a lunch date, did he sound as if he was in any trouble?" I asked.

"No!" Denny almost laughed. "Full of beans. Excited about a New York opening. They hadn't done any place in New York before. The Beaumont was a dream spot."

"Mentioned no quarrels with anyone?"

"Nothing at all like that. If he knew there was something up around the corner, it certainly wasn't bothering him very much," Denny said.

"So, later, he just came unexpectedly face to face with it," I commented.

"Those English kids?" Denny said.

I guess my face darkened. "Seven of them are alive and safe—on their way home," I said. "Four of them didn't make it. British government sent an air-force plane over to pick them up."

"But who freed them? The cops? Scotland Yard?" Denny asked.

"Chambrun," I said.

"Oh, wow! That's a story we'll want."

"You'll have to get it from him," I said.

So much for Frank Pasqua's lunch date. Nothing that helped. I tried to pry a name out of Denny—someone who might be close to Toby March and his troupe.

"Staying hidden is the name of March's game," Denny said.

"Some reporter who had done him a favor?" I asked.

"We all gave him the best break possible in the press."

"Pasqua was buying you lunch at the Spartan Bar. You must have been near the top of his life," I said.

"We started working on the same newspaper when we were first out of college. Our friendship had nothing to do with his success with Toby March. Not that I wasn't pleased for him that he had latched onto a real star. But we weren't friends because of it. It dates way back," Denny told Maggie and me.

"One of the things that is hard to understand," I said, "is that three people, very close to Toby—the girl he lives with, for God's sake, Colonel Watson, who took care of him in the hospital, Pasqua, his closest associate, all claim they can't say what he looks like without that mask."

"Don't forget," Denny said, "none of them knew him before the accident that destroyed his face. Millicent Huber and Watson were working in the hospital when he was brought in. He went to Frank Pasqua, his agent, when he was ready to leave the hospital and had already started the mask routine."

"It doesn't matter what he looked like before the plastic surgery. What does he look like now?"

Denny grinned at me. "I have seen him without the mask," he said.

"For God's sake, man, describe him!"

"I was having a drink with Frank in a bar in Phildelphia where we'd had one of our meetings. 'You've seen him,' Frank told me. 'He just walked by!'"

"'Where?' I wanted to know."

"Frank just shook his head. 'Part of my job is to keep his looks a secret,' he told me."

"So you saw him but you didn't see him," I said, "but Frank knows what he looks like?"

"Obviously."

"And he'd keep that secret, no matter what."

"To the grave," Denny said. "March knew he could be counted on all the way."

"To the grave is just where his loyalty may have taken him," I said.

Denny and Maggie Hanson both looked shocked. "You think—?" he asked.

"It's one of the theories that has been kicked around," I said. "Claridge, the Scotland Yard inspector who was killed, had come over from England because he thought March had something to do with the abduction of those British kids."

"Oh, wow!"

"He got into March's suite, 17C, and waited for him to come up from the show in the Blue Lagoon. But Frank Pasqua appeared first. He had an adjoining room to March's, and the hotel had fixed it so he could have access to March's suite. He came up to his room after the show—about two-thirty, was seen by our security. He went into 17C and there he finds a complete stranger, who turns out to be a Scotland Yard inspector. For the first time he hears that March may be involved with a kidnapping."

"What good will the kidnapping do March?" Denny asked.

"Three million bucks, and freedom for some Iranian terrorists. That meant all the legal investigation was pointed at Iran. Except Inspector Claridge's. When March turned in about three-thirty, he found Pasqua and Claridge waiting for him. Claridge lowered the boom and tried to make an arrest. March was ready for him, fought him off, killed him with a fireplace iron."

"And Frank?" Maggie Hanson asked in a shaking voice.

"Somebody was badly beaten in 17C," I said, "and bled like a stuck pig. It could have been Frank, it could have been March."

"Why would Toby attack Frank?" Maggie asked.

"Because Frank suddenly guessed the truth about Toby, and the eleven young hostages. He probably didn't know, though, that at least two of them were dead—a girl raped and slashed, a young man butchered like a fresh piece of meat. Tell me, Jack, would Frank Pasqua protect his friend against punishment for that kind of horror?"

Jack Denny looked as though I'd knocked him unconscious. "Never," he said. "He would keep a secret, a professional secret like what March really looks like, but cover for him in at least three murders—because, according to you, Claridge was lying there dead at their feet. I don't think he would have covered up for his own mother in such a situation. He hated physical violence. Even though March was his bread and butter, I'm certain he'd have turned him in."

"So I'm afraid you both have lost a cherished friend," I said.

"But why would March remove both bodies from his room?" Jack asked.

"There must not even be a whiff of a connection between March and the hostages. Claridge would provide that whiff. March must have been shaken by his dying friend. He took Frank away to give himself time to think about what to do with him," I replied.

"What to do?" Maggie asked.

"Finish killing him or letting him be found somewhere away from 17C," I said.

"But the blood was going to attract attention to 17C," Jack Denny said.

"He thought he had plenty of time to get to that," I said. "He had to move two grown men with people already up and around. Claridge was dead. He could be dumped in the basement—and was. Frank, I think, was still alive. March had to get him somewhere to care for him or kill him."

"Oh, my!" Maggie said. "But what about Frank's phone call to you, Mr. Haskell?"

"One of March's patented imitations," I said. "And it would stop us from looking for Frank. That 'unfinished business' routine was supposed to make us expect that Frank would show up when he finished doing something that was giving him pleasure."

Jack Denny squared his shoulders. "But this is all 'maybe,' isn't it?" he asked.

"Come up with something that fits the facts better," I suggested.

Neither one of them spoke. Maggie began to cry softly. I wanted to get back to Chambrun and tell how the new information I had discovered led to some pretty grim conclusions.

5

I was standing out in the lobby, looking around at what I think of as my world, although surely it was Chambrun's; it was invented by him, made to work by him.

But it hadn't been working in the last hours. There had been at least five murders: the four British hostages, Inspector Claridge, and possibly Frank Pasqua. And conceivably Toby March, if the facts turned around and, unlikely, Pasqua turned out to be the villain. And there was Betsy Ruysdale — Chambrun would give his own life, quickly and freely, to save her from death or torture.

Maggie Hanson had taken off for her apartment in Greenwich Village. "I simply can't accept the fact that Frank has been murdered," she told me. "I would *know* it! I would *feel* it." And so she left to wait for him to call her where he knew he could find her.

Jack Denny also departed. He had his job as a reporter to get rolling.

Guests circulated around the lobby and into the various

bars and lunchrooms. Among them, as invisible as if he weren't there, could be Toby March!

I decided to go find Chambrun and share some thoughts I had with him. I doubted my ideas would be startling revelations, though. He would, normally, be miles ahead of me, of any of us.

I took the service elevator up to Chambrun's office on the third floor. I knew Betsy wasn't going to be there, but I suppose I had some secret hopes. The person who was there, though, really surprised me.

Colonel Archibald Watson was sitting in Chambrun's chair. On the desk, in front of him, was the gun I had seen him carrying when they rescued the British kids. As I walked in, he reached for it. Then he smiled at me and drew back his hand.

"I agreed to stay here while Chambrun went up to his penthouse," he said. "We know someone is gunning for him, and we don't want anyone setting up an ambush while he is away."

"What about an ambush in the penthouse?" I asked.

"Jerry Dodd and a couple of his men went with him." He grinned at me. "Are you Toby March, sir?"

I didn't smile back. "You saw that carved-up boy," I said. "It's not easy to think of that as a funny question."

"Sorry," Watson said, "but that masked marvel has got us all acting a little crazy."

"Nothing on Betsy?" I asked him.

"No, I'm sorry to say," Watson said.

"No one has reported seeing her leave the lobby with a woman?" I asked.

"Seeing Betsy moving around with a possible guest isn't likely to attract special attention," Watson said.

"What did Chambrun need up in the penthouse?" I asked.

"Change of clothes, I think," Watson said.

I reached for the phone on the desk and dialed the penthouse. It rang several times before Chambrun answered. I felt relieved.

"I was worried about you," I said, "finding Watson here."

"With Betsy missing, it seemed to me that Watson, a man with a gun, was the best way not to find someone waiting for me when I came back," Chambrun said.

"What about Jerry Dodd or some of his men?" I asked.

"We're running out of men to look for people, and Watson likes action. I'll be down in a few minutes. Jerry's up here with me. Nothing to worry about."

"British kids gone?" Watson asked, when I hung up the phone.

"Supposed to be. I don't know for certain," I said.

Watson pointed to the phone as I put it down. "He's still convinced March is the villain of the piece," he said.

"But you're not?" I asked.

Watson shook his head. "No way. I know Toby. It's just not in the book for him to be it. Those kids saw those Iranian bastards butcher, rape, and kill. It was never just one man."

"One man in charge," I suggested.

"Can't Chambrun ever be wrong?" Watson asked.

"Not since I've known him."

"He should run for President," Watson said.

After a few minutes, one of Jerry Dodd's men came into the office. He looked around. "No one hidden in the closet?" he asked.

153

"Joke time again," Watson said.

Then Chambrun came in, looking his usual healthy, vibrant self. "Thanks for covering for me," he said to Watson. "No snoopers?"

"Haskell's been your only visitor," he said as he got up from the desk. "I'll go wander around."

"Why?" Chambrun asked.

Watson turned at the door and gave Chambrun an exasperated smile. "A man shoots at you on the roof, and misses killing you by the width of a hatband, and escapes."

"So?"

"So you know that action isn't finished. Why surround yourself with security? Why enlist me to guard your office? The terrorists who had those kids aren't going to give up. They still want three million dollars and their people freed."

"No judge or court in the world is going to free those four men we arrested with the hostages," Chambrun said. "Seven eyewitnesses to four murders!"

"But if they take you, there will be no problem about the money, and you should have influence enough in high places to get their compatriots released."

"I wish I were that important," Chambrun said, smiling.

"It doesn't matter whether you are or not," Watson said. "They *think* you are!"

"So he comes after me, wearing his mask—?"

Watson gave a sort of helpless shrug of his shoulders. "I wonder about your obsession with your Toby March theory," he said. "Is it that you can't bear not to have startling theories that differ from any normal one? This is still an Iran-oriented ball game. They want the people the British are holding. They want the four men we are holding turned loose. They never let down their friends. The British kids appeared to be sure-fire. You come next," Watson said.

"So why do you mingle among the people in the lobby?" Chambrun asked.

"It must be obvious that I might be helpful. I speak their language. I might hear someone talking, I might recognize a face. I knew some of the higher-ups pretty well. I could get lucky." He shook his head. "Why should I be concerned with protecting you? Because I wouldn't like to see anyone else get the drawn-and-quartered treatment those British kids got. If I had a chance to stop it, my conscience wouldn't let me not try."

"And you are convinced it's not Toby March?" Chambrun asked.

"Not Toby March alone, obviously. Those four guys who were holding the British youngsters make it certain that, if it is Toby March, he's not working alone."

"But Toby March doesn't have anything against me," Chambrun said. "I just gave him the best job he ever had. Two weeks in the Blue Lagoon."

"If he owes Iranian terrorists, he'll pay the price. He wants to live, I'm sure. You don't live if you cross those people."

"So I haven't crossed them," Chambrun said.

"You outwitted them. You found and freed the British kids. You're going to pay, they tell themselves, one way or the other. I'll see you around."

Watson looked at me. "Don't let him laugh this off, Haskell. It's not kid stuff. You know that. You've seen it."

I turned to Chambrun when the Colonel had gone. "He makes some sense," I said.

155

"I agree," Chambrun said, "but that doesn't erase Toby March from the scene. Toby March has been in charge of this operation for the terrorists from the beginning; from the original heisting of the British kids."

"Why would he bring them here to New York?"

"Obvious. He had an appointment here as a musician. If he didn't show up for it, it would just about wipe out his musical future. He had to have the hostages where he could keep his finger on them. Then the whole thing went sour when I got into the act, throwing suspicion on him, and I had to be added to his targets. Watson's gone out there to listen for some Iranian voices. There is another sound he might hear—Toby March's voice."

"He doesn't know what he looks like, but he might know what he sounds like?" I asked.

"So might a lot of others around here," Chambrun said. "Millicent Huber, March's musicians, Frank Pasqua, if he's alive."

"But would any of them turn him in if they spotted him?" I asked.

"Not likely," Chambrun said. "Whatever are the true facts about March, one is quite certain. He manages to instill a special loyalty in his friends."

"And a share of three million bucks, if you're right," I said.

"And where is he going to get three million dollars?"

"From you, if you're his next victim," I said.

"I wish I knew how to raise three million dollars for me," Chambrun said. "If I knew how, I'd have done it long ago."

"You know perfectly well that if you disappeared and a demand for that much money was made for your return, there would be no problem finding it." And I meant it.

"So now?" I asked.

"We wait for someone else to make a move," he said.

A break in the fog came sooner than we could have expected, and in a far more unpleasant way. A certified letter for Chambrun, delivered by a carefully identified post office employee. The letter laid it on the line, unhappily.

Chambrun:

You can only avoid this for a very short time. The stakes are still the same—three million dollars in British pounds, and our four men you recently arrested. What you will get in return is Miss Ruysdale. I may tell you, she isn't enjoying what is happening to her now. Later will be worse.

There was no signature.

Chambrun brought his fist down on his desk. His face was suddenly the color of parchment. "I was hoping against hope this wasn't the way it would happen," he almost shouted. He turned to Lieutenant Herzog, who had come up with the man from the post office. "I'll do what I can about the money, Lieutenant. See what you can do about getting those four creeps released from jail."

"Let me warn you, Chambrun, the chance of getting that to happen is smaller than you can imagine," Herzog said.

"Not to save a woman's life? Not for Betsy?"

"I think it would take an order from the President," Herzog said.

"Then *ask* him!"

"So what do we have?" Herzog asked. "Miss Ruysdale was seen walking out of the lobby with a woman."

"Which may have no connection whatever with this," Chambrun said, shaking the typewritten letter in the air.

"That could have been some ordinary hotel business," Herzog said. "March and company caught up with her later."

"He hasn't shown up or communicated with us, has he?" Chambrun's voice was loud and unsteady. Betsy was the closest person in the world to him. "Get all his people here, will you, Lieutenant. The four musicians, Watson, and Miss Huber. They may be able to tell us something about his habits that would give us a lead. Betsy has been gone less than an hour. March had to write this letter after she was taken, get it to the post office, get it delivered. Betsy can't be too far away."

Herzog left to find the people Chambrun wanted to see. I couldn't decide whether I'd be more useful staying with Chambrun or joining in the roundup, I had a feeling he was torn between not wanting to be alone and showing his emotions, even to someone close like me.

The four young musicians were the first of March's group to be brought to the office. Their first concern was for March. Would he show up for tonight's performance? Their jobs, their bread and butter, depended on that. They had nothing of any use to us. They had no social contact with March whatever. They worked with him on musical arrangements and nothing else. They didn't even have a drink with him after a show, wherever they were playing. What kind of a man was he? They really couldn't say. He was a brilliant musician, a perfectionist, but what he was like as a man was a mystery to them. A man in a mask. Nothing to reveal any emotion of any kind. He'd never mentioned friends in New York or anywhere else except once; there had been an explanation of Millicent Huber. She'd been a nurse in the hospital where he'd had his plastic surgery done. They'd become close. That was all.

The Scotland Yard inspector arrived as Chambrun was finishing his fruitless questioning of the young musicians.

"Herzog has just told me about Miss Ruysdale," he said. "I can't tell you how sorry I am, Mr. Chambrun."

"If that would help, I'd thank you," Chambrun said, his voice bitter.

"I may have some help for you in a little while," the inspector said.

"A little while isn't soon enough," Chambrun said.

"One of the doctors who did the plastic surgery on March in the London hospital is on his way here. He must have a history on March, and probably a description of him before and after the operation."

"That would be something," Chambrun conceded. "But when will he get here?"

The inspector glanced at his wristwatch. "About an hour," he said. "Can you meet any of the terms in the letter?"

"The money, possibly," Chambrun said. "Freedom for four murderers is something else again. Would your government do anything about the terrorists they are holding?"

"I doubt it," the inspector said. "It isn't their style to give in to blackmailers."

"Probably not mine, either," Chambrun said. "It's easy to be strong when the person in danger doesn't mean anything to you."

"You must have some friends with influence who could appeal to them," the inspector said. "Over the years, you must have done favors for people who can wield some influence."

"Like giving someone a special suite, or a special, imported bottle of wine, or tickets to a theater that is reportedly sold out. Would they help Betsy because of things like that?" Chambrun asked.

"You won't know till you try," the inspector said. "That's where I think you should be headed. When Dr. Cuyler gets here, I'll bring him directly to you."

The inspector left us. Chambrun sat at his desk, pounding down on it with both fists. "I just sit here, doing nothing, while God only knows what that bastard is doing to Betsy."

"I've been thinking of Judge Norton," I said. Judge David Norton was on the court of appeals. About a year back, his son had been arrested on a drug charge. Chambrun had helped prove the boy innocent and provided information that led the police to the real criminal. I had heard the judge tell Chambrun that he owed a debt that he might never be able to pay. He might be helpful now getting four killers released.

"He will only tell me how sorry he is that he can't maneuver us around the law," Chambrun said.

"Worth a try?" I asked.

Chambrun reached out a hand to me. "See if you can locate him. Tell him what the score is. I'll be here, trying to raise the money."

160

Chambrun was going to try to be ready to give in to the blackmailer, or blackmailers, if he had to, for Betsy's sake. He must be feeling, I thought, pretty much the way the parents of those British kids had felt when they got the same kind of demand. You stand tough until someone you love is the target.

As I left his office, I saw him slip that pistol into his jacket pocket. If it came down to it, he was ready to kill for Betsy.

I had been very close to the situation when Chambrun helped Judge Norton with his son's problem. The day was over and the judge would probably be at his club, having supper and drinks with friends. I called him there, and he sounded heartily cheerful when he answered.

"Hi, Mark. Nice to hear from you. You around here somewhere? I'll buy you a drink."

I told him I was at the hotel in New York. "Chambrun has big trouble and could use your help," I said. "It's too complex for me to explain on the phone."

"Take me forty-five minutes to get there," Norton said. "Tell Pierre I'm on my way."

I had hoped and expected he would answer that way. Lieutenant Herzog came into my private office. "You have any idea where Colonel Watson and Miss Huber might be?" he asked. "They are not in the colonel's room, and no one has seen them about."

"They were going to wander around," I said, "looking for some sign of an Iranian presence."

"So we don't know where to look?" Herzog asked.

"I don't know, certainly."

I joined Chambrun to let him know Judge Norton was on his way. He looked relieved.

"The money is going to be possible," he said, "but getting it in British pounds is not so simple before tomorrow."

"They'll know that," I said.

"You mean, March will know that."

"You're still convinced about him?"

"Positive," Chambrun said.

If Judge Norton had been operating on a time schedule, he couldn't have been more accurate. It was just forty-seven minutes after our phone conversation that he walked into Chambrun's office.

They greeted each other warmly. Then Chambrun began to tell him what had been happening.

"I know about the British kids," Norton said, "and that you rescued them. Bravo!"

"Now it is another situation and far more personally painful," Chambrun said. He went into the story about Betsy and the blackmail letter.

The judge's face darkened. "How are you supposed to get the money to them?" he asked.

"Earlier instructions," Chambrun said. "We turn the four Iranian killers loose, give one of them three million dollars in British pounds, and wait for them to keep their word and turn Betsy free."

"I can guess why you sent for me," Norton said. "Some way to free those killers?"

Chambrun nodded.

The judge shook his snow-white head. "You are about as likely to get an order for that as you are to land a date with the President's lady," he said.

"But Betsy—?"

"Let me think a minute," the judge said. "The prosecutor who gets those four men, involved in the murder of those English kids, electrocuted will become a national hero. The man who signs an order to set them free will be hooted out of American politics. I know if I had the power to sign an order that would set them free, I wouldn't sign it."

"Not to free Betsy?"

"I'm afraid not, Pierre. Those English parents are entitled to justice, too."

"So thanks for nothing," Chambrun said angrily.

"I didn't say I wouldn't help, Pierre," the judge said. "Now suppose," he continued, "it was decided to move those four murderers who are being held, from where they are now, to another jail. And suppose in the process of the move they escape?"

"They wouldn't move them without an army," Chambrun said.

"I know," the judge said. "But before they were moved out of the jail, they could be left alone together in a room somewhere. According to the accounts I've heard, you have a man who speaks their language."

"Colonel Watson," I said.

"He could be gotten in to see those criminals, and tell them what to expect and what to do, when and how."

"That means someone guarding the prisoners has to play it your way," Chambrun said.

"I know," the judge said. "But for Betsy, he might be willing to look careless, and not callous."

"But who will that person be?"

"That's where I may be able to help," the judge answered.

"Have your colonel ready, and when I learn what he has to know, he'll have to be ready to move quickly."

"Count on it," Chambrun said. "But I don't understand how you can wangle this, David."

"English connections," the judge said. "They will ask me to represent them in some aspect of the case. I will need the prisoners moved to some place where I can work with a translator. We lose them in the process."

"How good a chance is there that it will work?" Chambrun asked.

"Better than you ought to believe, I suppose," the judge said, smiling. "I think you can assume that Betsy will be safe until you fail to produce for them, which can't happen until tomorrow."

"Those bastards raped one of the English girls," Chambrun said.

"I may sound unfeeling to you, Pierre. It's nasty to think that might happen to Betsy, but if she comes out all in one piece, can it matter to you? She'll be the same Betsy, just as true and faithful to you as she's ever been. Hang tight in there, friend." And the judge turned and left.

"Find Watson," Chambrun said to me.

"I was looking for him when I thought of the judge," I said. "Watson is apparently still in the lobby."

"There is no need for him to keep looking for Iranians," Chambrun said. "While they have Betsy, we can't lift a finger against them."

"Do you really think they'll set her free if you come through with what they are asking for?"

"He shook his head slowly from side to side. "Who can say for sure?" he said.

The office door opened, and our Scotland Yard friend came in, accompanied by a nice-looking middle-aged man with smartly barbered blond hair. He was introduced to us as Dr. Cuyler, the surgeon from the London hospital.

"Sudden trip, Doctor," Chambrun said.

"As you Americans say, 'You can say that again,' " Dr. Cuyler said.

"We are getting to know your hospital well," Chambrun said. "We already have two of your alumni here—Colonel Watson and Millicent Huber."

The doctor's face hardened. "I'll be glad to see Watson," he said. "He walked out on us without any notice. He had a responsible job, and we had no chance to replace him before his sudden exit."

"You were involved in the surgery on Toby March?" Chambrun asked.

"I assisted the head surgeon," Dr. Cuyler said.

"Can you give us a physical description of him?"

"Six feet tall, well-muscled body, talented musician."

"You've heard him perform?"

"Not what he's doing now," Dr. Cuyler said, "the imitations that have made him famous. When he was recovering in the hospital, he used to get to the piano in the recreation room. He had been performing all over Europe and Asia; not famous, but busy. His face was such a mess, he knew he couldn't appear in public anymore.

" 'I'll pretend to be someone else,' he said. And then he started to do an imitation of Frank Sinatra. It was amazingly good. The next time I saw him, he had bought a mask. He did a Bing Crosby for me. He had it made, I knew."

"But what did his face look like?" Chambrun asked.

"At that time, it was a butcher's counter. When he could be released, he still had no face that could be recognized by a close friend. The Huber woman had fallen in love with him in the process of caring for him. She left the hospital with him when he left. To care for him, help him get going."

"She and Watson came over here to be present at his opening here in the hotel," Chambrun said. "The Beaumont was a top date for him. If you saw him now, could you identify him?"

"Perhaps if I could examine his face closely, I could see where skin grafts took place, and I'd know."

"You may get that chance," Chambrun said, his voice grim. "He's somewhere not too far away. I think I know where."

"Chambrun!" I said.

"I'm afraid I've been slow on the uptake, Mark," Chambrun said. "He's been right in my hands and I let him slip through. Now he's got Betsy."

The office door opened and Colonel Watson and Millicent Huber came in.

"Herzog said you have been looking for me," Watson said.

"Something new," he said. "Some way to find Miss Ruysdale."

"Something like that," Chambrun said. "This is Dr. Cuyler. I suspect you know him from your old hospital in London."

"I don't know this man," Dr. Cuyler said.

"Why, this is Colonel Watson," Chambrun said.

"The devil he is!" Dr. Cuyler said. "I've never seen this man before."

"Of course he hasn't, has he, Toby?" Chambrun said.

I looked around, expected to see someone else in the room. Chambrun was looking directly at Watson—and he had called him "Toby."

The man I knew as Watson moistened his lips. "You flipped your lid, Chambrun?" he asked. He didn't quite sound the way he had before. His British accent seemed to have thinned out.

"I should have guessed quite a while back," Chambrun said. "A television studio has been trying to prepare a show based on the Beaumont, and they were looking for an actor to play Pierre Chambrun. They sent me half a dozen tapes of a show called 'Magnum P.I.' There's an actor who plays an Englishman. I think his name is John Hillerman. The Englishman's name is Higgins. It's that voice you have been using as Colonel Watson, isn't it, Toby? Only a fluent imitator could have copied that voice so perfectly."

"You must be off your rocker, Chambrun," the man, whoever he was, said.

"I've been off my rocker not to have identified you from the start," Chambrun said.

"Can you prove all this, Mr. Chambrun?" the Scotland Yard inspector asked.

"I think Dr. Cuyler can prove it if he gets a close look at Toby's face."

Cuyler took a step forward.

"Stay away from me, Doc," the man said. His hand crept toward his pocket. Chambrun was quicker. His pistol was aimed directly at March. It had to be March if Chambrun said so.

"You have three matters to settle, March," Chambrun said.

167

"Where is Betsy? What happened to Colonel Watson? What happened to Frank Pasqua? And if Betsy isn't returned in one piece, you are going to die more painfully than you can imagine."

"Take it easy, Mr. Chambrun," the inspector said.

"There comes a time when you don't take it easy," Chambrun said, "when you are dealing with a monster."

March turned and started for the door. Chambrun fired his gun. March must have heard the bullet go past his ear before it buried itself in the door.

"I never miss except on purpose, March," Chambrun said. "Let's take a quick look at things."

March turned slowly back. Beads of sweat glistened on his forehead.

"Before your accident, you were performing in Iran," Chambrun said. "You were persuaded to take charge of their hostage-taking plans."

"Why would he get involved with this terrorism," I asked, "when he was already making a small fortune as an entertainer?"

"Maybe he got to like the taste of blood," Chambrun said. "Is that how it was, March? Three million struck me as an odd amount, but now I think I understand it. One million to his terrorist allies, one million to Miss Huber, and the third million for himself. Is that how it was to be, March?"

March just stared back.

"That brought you back to England," Chambrun continued, "to handle the taking of those eleven British kids. You must have had to communicate with your Iranian partners. The real Colonel Watson overheard or discovered what you were up to, so he is dead. I suspect Scotland Yard will find his body at the bottom of the Thames. Then you came over here to fulfill your musical obligations. The hostages were brought here, with a small army to keep watch for you. Inspector Claridge found out the truth sooner than any of the rest of us. He died, and Frank Pasqua witnessed his killing. He had to die, too, even though he was your close friend. Where will we find him? In the East River or the Hudson? Now, Betsy is either where I think she is, or you are a dead man!"

"Where do you think she is?" March asked.

"The one place where you were sure we wouldn't look. The house down the street where you held the hostages. We went over it from roof to basement, so you think we have no reason to go back there. Is that where she is, March?"

"This whole fairy tale is going to make you a laughing-stock," March said.

"You want to tell me, Miss Huber? You lured Betsy out of the hotel so some of March's boys could take care of her."

Millicent Huber was crying, shaking her head from side to side.

"The only thing there will be to laugh at is your body and Miss Huber's body riddled with bullets," Chambrun said to March.

He turned to me. "Find Herzog, Mark. I want him and three or four men to go with me down the street." Chambrun looked at the inspector and said, "I trust you to hold this man here."

"I don't have any authority to—"

"You have the authority of one caring human being,"

Chambrun said. "Do you have a gun? Give him your gun, Mark. You're not going to need it."

Chambrun and I went down to the lobby, where we found Herzog and told him the score. He got four of his men and we headed, almost running, down the street to where the young British hostages had been held.

"If she's guarded, we're out of luck," Herzog said when he tried the locked door, "if we make any noise."

There were no lights visible in the house.

"I live in a world of locked rooms," Chambrun said. "You think I can't open a lock quietly?" He took his penknife out of his pocket. There was some kind of tool on it in addition to the blades. In a matter of seconds, the front door to the house was open. No lights on inside. No sound of any kind.

Chambrun reached out and felt along the wall, found a light switch, and the room was illuminated. It was the room where the British hostages had been held and butchered. It was empty now—except for Betsy.

Chambrun uttered a little cry of relief. She was propped against the wall, eyes wide open, a gag over her mouth, her arms tied behind her, and her legs tied at the ankles.

Chambrun ran to her. I stood with the four cops by the door. Chambrun knelt and took the gag from her mouth.

"Millicent Huber," she said. "She told me there was something wrong in one of the ladies' rooms, and when she got me there, she pulled a gun on me."

"Don't worry, love," Chambrun said. "She's under arrest, along with Toby March."

"You found him? How?"

"I got smart, almost too late," Chambrun said. "Colonel Watson is—or was—Toby March."

"Oh, my gosh!" Betsy said.

Chambrun untied her wrists and ankles and then he took her in his arms and kissed her tenderly on the lips. She pulled back after a moment, and looked at me and the cops over his shoulder.

"Are you going public on us, Pierre?" she asked.

He kissed her again. "Now and forever!" he said.